CARRY ON

JONATHAN D. DORFMAN

www.dizzyemupublishing.com

DIZZY EMU PUBLISHING
1714 N McCadden Place, Hollywood, Los Angeles 90028
www.dizzyemupublishing.com

Carry On
Jonathan D. Dorfman

ISBN: 9798636854807

First published in the United States
in 2020 by Dizzy Emu Publishing

www.dizzyemupublishing.com

CARRY ON

JONATHAN D. DORFMAN

<u>CARRY ON</u>

Written by

Jonathan D. Dorfman

I/E. EDNA'S CAR - AFTERNOON

JUDE DUNN (JD), 17, sits shotgun while HIS MOTHER, EDNA, 42,
drives. JD wears jeans and a black T-shirt that reads "THE
NITRO PUMPKINS" with a picture of an exploding jack-o'-
lantern. Edna wears a red dress.

                         EDNA
                  So, how was your day? Anything
                  interesting happen?

JD tilts his head to the side.

                         JD
                  There was a fight in the cafeteria.

                         EDNA
                  On the first day?

                         JD
                  I know, right?

                         EDNA
                  How'd it happen?

                                                    CUT TO:

INT. HARTFORD HIGH SCHOOL - CAFETERIA - AFTERNOON

JD and RICKY MALLO stand in front of each other. The
cafeteria is packed. Everybody watches them, holding their
lunches. A few people drop their lunches.

                         JD
                  Say it again. Say it again, I dare
                  you. I double dare you,
                  motherfucker! Say it one more God
                  damn time!

Ricky shrugs and looks JD square in the eyes.

                         RICKY
                  Ass-burger.

                                                    BACK TO:

I/E. EDNA'S CAR - PRESENT

JD still sits in his mother's car. The light turns red, and
Mrs. Dunn stops in traffic.

                    EDNA
          Cut to the end, Jules. How'd it
          end?

                    JD
          Well...

                                        CUT TO:

INT. HARTFORD HIGH SCHOOL - CAFETERIA - AFTERNOON

JD punches Ricky to the ground.

                    JD
          Do I look like a bitch? Is that all
          I am to you? Answer the question!
          Do I look like a bitch to you?

A smug grin crosses Ricky's bloody face.

                    RICKY
          Huh, yeah.

                    JD
          I am nobody's bitch!

The lunch monitors hold JD back from stomping on Ricky.

                                        BACK TO:

I/E. EDNA'S CAR - PRESENT

The light is now green, and cars honk behind the Dunns. Mrs.
Dunn looks at her son horrified. Her jaw is agape.

                    JD
          Green, Mom.

                    EDNA
          The hell am I going to do with you?

A car honks its horn again, and Mrs. Dunn takes off.

                    JD
          So, remember how I wasn't going to
          land myself in detention this year?

                    EDNA
          Yes, I remember.

                    JD
          It's a suspension, now. The good
          news is they didn't call the police
          this time.

                                        CUT TO:

INT. HARTFORD HIGH SCHOOL - DR. TOLINI'S OFFICE - EARLIER

JD sits across from the principal, DR. TOLINI, 49. Dr. Tolini
is a tall, muscular, African-American man with a deep voice.
His office is cozy; not large, but not cramped, either.

                    DR. TOLINI
          Mr. Dunn. We need to stop meeting
          like this. I'll let you off with
          just two detentions... this time.
          If you assault another student, we
          will be forced to charge you with
          such.

                    JD
          Detention? Don't you think you're a
          little uptight?

Dr. Tolini raises an eyebrow.

                    JD
          You know what you could use right
          now?

                    DR. TOLINI
          Please enlighten me, Mr. Dunn.

                    JD
          You need to go out, find a nice
          girl, have a nice screw... Maybe
          even...

                    DR. TOLINI
          Mr. Dunn! That is inappropriate!

                    JD
               (singing)
          What do you get when you fall in
          love?
               (spoken)
          Eh... I'd say about five, no! Six
          months of penicillin shots. It's
          like an adventure!

                    DR. TOLINI
          That's enough, JD.

                    JD
          Hey, I hear Nurse Linda has a
          wandering eye for you...

                    DR. TOLINI
          You're trying my patience...

                    JD
          Naw, I'm trying to dig myself out
          of a hole.

                    DR. TOLINI
          Allow me to put you back in it. Two
          days suspension. If you're lucky, I
          may just forget about the
          detentions.

                    JD
          Hey, maybe we'll both get lucky...

JD clicks and winks. Dr. Tolini still scowls.

                    DR. TOLINI
          Do I look amused to you, Mr. Dunn?

                    JD
          No, but you should...

Dr. Tolini glares.

                    JD
          Is joke, you laugh, "ha, ha!" Is
          funny, no?

                    DR. TOLINI
          No. Go home, JD.

                    JD
          See, we're at a first name basis
          again. You're gonna miss me when
          I'm gone.

                    DR. TOLINI
          Just... Go. Please. I need headache
          medicine.

                    JD
          Oh, like Mom? She usually drinks a
          fifth.

                                        CUT TO:

I/E. EDNA'S CAR - PRESENT

Edna sits at a stop sign, looking in awe at her son. Angry
drivers shake their fists and honk behind her.

                         DRIVER
               Move it, Lady! You've been sitting
               there for ten minutes!

                         EDNA
               You're unbelievable. I thought you
               were past this, Jude. I'm trying so
               hard to show you appropriate
               behavior, and you go and do this.

                         JD
               I'm trying, too. And I'm failing.
               And I'm sorry.

Mrs. Dunn and Jude look at each other for a beat.

                         JD
               I should've gone for refuge in
               audacity.

                         EDNA
               I know you took your meds today. I
               watched you. What's going through
               your head, right now?

JD opens his mouth and closes it, again.

                         EDNA
               Well?

                         JD
               A bunch of fired neurons, racing
               all over the place.

                         EDNA
               Jude, I'm not in the mood!

                         JD
               I got nothing.

                         EDNA
               That's for sure.

The Dunns pull into their driveway. A street sign reads
"SENTRY RD."

EXT. THE DUNNS' FRONT YARD - AFTERNOON

JD and his mother exit the car, a red Toyota. Their next door neighbor, JACK GLADWYNNE, looks up from pruning his prized bushes. They are shaped like lions and tigers. Jack is currently working on a bear.

                    JACK GLADWYNNE
          Hey, Edna! Hey, Jude!

                    EDNA
          Hi, Jack.

                    JACK GLADWYNNE
          Don't say that on a plane.

Jack laughs. Edna doesn't.

                    JACK GLADWYNNE
          Rough day?

                    EDNA
          You could say that.

                    JD
          Not as rough as it was for Ricky.

                    EDNA
          Jude, that's enough.

                    JD
          To be fair, Ricky started it.

                    EDNA
          I don't care who started it. You're
          not going to end it. Am I clear?

                    JD
          Actually, I think you're a bit red
          in the face, right now.

                    EDNA
          I give up.

A beat.

                    EDNA
          What's the theme for this year?

                    JACK GLADWYNNE
          Homages to George Takei. You know,
          "lions and tigers and bears. Ohh
          myyyyy..."

JD GROANS while Edna looks confused.

                    JACK GLADWYNNE
          Don't worry about it. Just a bad
          pun.

                    JD
          Bad doesn't even describe it!

                    EDNA
          Get inside, NOW.

                    JD
          I think the "red shirts" are
          rolling in their graves.

                    EDNA
          Now.

                    JD
          Why don't you like fun?

Edna glares at JD, as he trudges inside the house.

                    EDNA
          I don't know what to do with him.

                    JACK GLADWYNNE
          He really seemed to take the news
          pretty hard. Father skippin' out on
          his high school graduation. I'd be
          upset, too.

                    EDNA
          We already explained to him that he
          didn't have a choice. Bill's job
          requires him to go on tour that
          month.

                    JACK GLADWYNNE
          True, but do you really think he's
          going to let go of it anytime soon?
          Look at it from his perspective.

Edna stands still and tilts her head for a moment.

                                        CUT TO:

INT. THE DUNNS' LIVING ROOM - EVENING

Bill and Edna stand before JD, who sits on the couch.

                    JD
          So, let me get this straight: You
          can go to Bernadette's graduation,
          but you can't attend mine.

                    BILL
          Jude, I know you're upset by this,
          but...

                    JD
          This is hardly fucking fair! She's
          always been your favorite!

                    EDNA
          That's not true.

                    JD
          I mean, I'm sorry I'm not a perfect
          little angel like her, but God!
          What do I have to do to get your
          attention around here?

                    EDNA
          Ho! You have our attention, all
          right. Believe me, nobody can miss
          you.

                    JD
          What's that supposed to mean?

                    EDNA
          Like the time you tried to push
          your father off a second floor
          balcony.

                    JD
          Hey! He landed in the pool.

                    BILL
          Or the time you decided to play
          "sword fight" with Bernadette.

                    JD
          How was I supposed to know that
          security had us on tape?

                    EDNA
          Two words: New. Zealand.

JD shudders.

                    BILL
          Now, I'm going on tour whether you
          like it or not.

> There's nothing you can say or do
> that will change that. Go upstairs,
> calm down, and go to bed. You have
> school tomorrow.

                    JD
          Make me.

Edna raises an eyebrow at JD.

                    JD
          I'll be good.

                                        CUT TO:

EXT. THE DUNNS' FRONT YARD

Jack Gladwynne raises an eyebrow at Edna.

                    EDNA
          Okay, so it could have gone
          better... But hey! That doesn't
          excuse his behavior today.

                    JACK GLADWYNNE
          I never said it did.

INT. THE DUNNS' HOUSE - MOMENTS LATER

Edna walks through the front door. She walks through the
house to...

THE BASEMENT

BILL DUNN, 45, sits at a computer station with many monitors.
He has turned their basement into a recording studio. JD sits
with him, both of them wearing large headphones.

                    EDNA
          Guys?

Bill and JD remove their headphones.

                    BILL
          Oh! Hi, Sweetie. We were just
          listening to one of my latest
          recordings for the tour.

                    EDNA
          Jude, can you go upstairs for a
          second. I need to talk to your
          father.

                    JD
          Uh-oh.

JD gets out of his seat and walks to the stairs. He passes by
a keyboard and taps Chopin's "Funeral March," eventually
making his way up the steps.

                    EDNA
          Very funny, Jude.

Bill spins around in his chair to face Edna. He is wearing a
gray T-shirt under a blue unbuttoned shirt and jeans.

                    BILL
          Um... Should I ask what that was
          about?

                    EDNA
          Jude got into a fight in the
          cafeteria today.

                    BILL
          Did he win?

                    EDNA
          Yes, and the prize was a
          suspension.

                    BILL
          Wow, day damn one. Impressive.

                    EDNA
          Bill!

                    BILL
          So, now what? I mean, what do we do
          about it?

                    EDNA
          Well, I was thinking you two should
          try some father-son bonding. Maybe
          you could teach him about the
          guitar. Perhaps if he's not as mad
          at you, he won't act out so much.

                    BILL
          Worth a shot.

A beat.

                    BILL
          I'll take him to Dim Witty's.

INT. THE DUNNS' HOUSE - KITCHEN - MOMENTS LATER

JD stands with the fridge open.

                    JD
          Ah. Cool air and Kool-Aid. A
          winning combination.

Bill and Edna walk up the steps into the kitchen.

                    BILL
          C'mon, Sport. We're going to get
          you a guitar.

                    JD
          Should I be scared? Is this a trap?

                    BILL
          Naw, Jude. Put your Kool-Aid in a
          bottle, and let's go.

                    JD
          I'm getting committed, aren't I?
          What color wallet do you want, Mom?

                    BILL
          You're not getting committed. I
          just wanna spend some quality time
          with my son before I go out on
          tour. Is that a crime?

                    JD
          Sure you don't want a wallet, Mom?

                    BILL
          Why don't we talk about it in the
          car?

Bill ushers JD out of the kitchen.

                    JD
               (singing)
          They're coming to take me away! Ha,
          ha!

I/E. BILL'S CAR - AFTERNOON

Bill drives with JD sitting shotgun. JD fidgets and taps on
the arm rest.

                    BILL
          Something you wanna talk about?

                    JD
          Why aren't you guys yelling?

                    BILL
          Jude, no amount of yelling is going
          to get you to stop being angry. So,
          why don't we focus that energy into
          something constructive?

                    JD
          Like what?

INT. DIM WITTY'S MUSIC STORE - MOMENTS LATER

JD stands in awe as Bill pays for something just out of view.

                    JD
          You're nuts! N- V- T- S, NUTS!
          Mom'll kill you!

                    BILL
          This was Mom's idea.

The clerk hands a Gibson Les Paul to Bill. The guitar is
green and shiny. A dangling price tag reveals its expensive
cost: $1,995.99. JD stumbles back and nearly faints.

EXT. DIM WITTY'S MUSIC STORE - PARKING LOT - MOMENTS LATER

JD and Bill walk through the packed parking lot. Bill carries
a guitar case in his hand.

                    BILL
          We are going to make you a great
          guitarist.

                    JD
          But I've only ever played keys.

                    BILL
          True, which is why I'm going to
          teach you the guitar. As long as
          you have all that energy to spend,
          right?

                    JD
          Do I even know you?

They reach Bill's black Hyundai.

                    BILL
          Son, rest assured, there will be
          consequences for your actions in
          the cafeteria today. Clearly, us
          yelling at you isn't working. So,
          your mom and I figured...

                    JD
          Figured what? That you can buy my
          emotions with a guitar?

                    BILL
          No. Listen, Jude. Your anger is
          well deserved, but you need to keep
          it under control. Put that energy
          to better use. Make something of
          it. That's all we're saying.

                    JD
          Dad... I, I just can't believe
          you're choosing Brock over me. I
          have issues with that.

                    BILL
          Let's look at it this way. You want
          me to be there for you. I want to
          keep a roof over your head and food
          on your plate. Life isn't always
          fair. In order to meet my goal, you
          need to postpone your goal a little
          bit.

JD gets in the shotgun seat and sulks, looking away from
Bill.

                    JD
          Whatev.

He slams the door with a loud WHAM.

Bill SIGHS.

INT. THE BASEMENT - LATER

Bill and JD sit on stools. Bill holds his guitar, while JD
holds the guitar Bill just bought him.

                    BILL
          Now, play an E-Minor Chord just
          like I taught you.

JD strums, and it sounds nothing like an E-Minor Chord.

                    JD
          This is useless! This is just going
          to piss me off even more.

                    BILL
          Take a deep breath, and calm down.
          Imagine how much more awesome it's
          going to feel when you nail it.

                    JD
          Dad, we've been down here for two
          hours. Let's face it; I'm never
          going to be awesome.

                    BILL
          You expect to be awesome in just
          two hours?

Bill stares at JD. JD stares back for a moment, looks at his
guitar, and sighs.

                    BILL
          Well?

                    JD
          No, Dad.

                    BILL
          Why don't we take a break?

INT. HARTFORD HIGH SCHOOL - MR. D.'S CLASS - MORNING

MR. D., 56, leans against his desk, drinking from a mug of
coffee. JD and Ricky sit before him.

                    MR. D.
          These games have gone far enough,
          you two. If you want to graduate
          this year, I'd recommend you cut
          the crap and learn to be civil with
          each other.

JD and Ricky glare at each other.

                    MR. D.
          You're almost grown adults. I'm not
          saying you have to like each other,
          but you don't have to make each
          other's lives harder than they need
          to be. Are we clear?

                    JD AND RICKY
               (in unison)
          Yes.

                    MR. D.
          Good. I'm glad we could have this
          talk.

More students pile into the classroom. One of them, AMY
GLADWYNNE, 16, catches JD's eye.

                    MR. D.
          Guys, meet our new friend joining
          us, Amy Gladwynne.

                    AMY
          Hi. I just moved here from
          Nashville. My mom's sick, so I'm
          staying with my uncle and aunt 'til
          she's better.

                    MR. D.
          I hope you all will show Amy the
          same kind of support you show each
          other.

JD hears words flying around the room, but he doesn't listen
to them. All he is focused on is Amy.

                    AMY
          Blah blah-blah blee-blah.

                    MR. D.
          Blah, blah-by blah.

                    RICKY
          Blah. Blah. Blah? JD!

Ricky nudges him. JD almost clings to the ceiling.

                    RICKY
          You're up, dude.

                    JD
          What're we doing again?

                    RICKY
          We're introducing ourselves. If you
          want, you can go back on screen
          saver mode. I can introduce you to
          the class. All I'd have to say is
          that you're an autistic ass.

                    JD
          I'd rather be an ass than a douche-
          canoe like you, Dick.

JD and Ricky glare at each other with lightning shooting from
their eyes.

                    MR. D.
          Knock it off, you two.

JD and Ricky look away from each other, sulking.

EXT. HARTFORD HIGH SCHOOL - AFTERNOON

JD walks alone. Amy walks up behind him.

                    AMY
          Hey!

JD startles and trips over his own two feet.

                    AMY
          Oh, my goodness! Are you okay?

                    JD
          Peachy.

JD pulls himself up and dusts himself off.

                    AMY
          What's up with Ricky? He was such a
          jack-ass to you, earlier.

                    JD
          He's always a jack-ass. Why do you
          think his name's Dick?

Amy laughs.

                    AMY
          You have an interesting way with
          words.

                    JD
          What's interesting about it?

JD stares at Amy, while she laughs.

                    JD
          What?

                    AMY
          Mind if I walk with you?

                    JD
          Okay.

JD and Amy walk as they talk.

                    AMY
          So where do you live?

                    JD
          Right around the corner.

                    AMY
          You don't really talk much, do you?

                    JD
          What do you mean?

                    AMY
          In class, you hardly said a word.

                    JD
          So?

                    AMY
          You're hardly talking now.

                    JD
          And?

                    AMY
          That's not very sociable of a
          gentleman.

                    JD
          Huh?

                    AMY
          I just meant that you're a man is
          all.

                    JD
          I am?

JD and Amy round the corner onto...

THE DUNNS' FRONT YARD

                    AMY
          I can't tell if you're funny or
          just a smart-ass.

                    JD
          I'm an Aspie. If that helps.

                    AMY
          Dear Lord. I traded Nashville for
          this.

Amy walks ahead with a huff.

                    JD
          Was it something I said?

INT. HARTFORD HIGH SCHOOL - MUSIC CLASS - AFTERNOON

JD sits at a table with his group, NICK MACCLOUD, 18, and
JOHN HAMMEL, 18. Nick wears jeans and a flannel shirt with
the sleeves rolled up. John sits opposite from JD and Nick,
frowning. The teacher, MR. SPEIGEL, 45, addresses the class.

                    MR. SPEIGEL
          I'm sure you all heard the rumors.
          FME Records and VH1 are, in fact,
          seeking talented graduating seniors
          for a new reality series. I am told
          there will be a talent competition
          in March to select three acts for
          the show.

Nick raises his hand.

                    MR. SPEIGEL
          Yes, Mr. MacCloud.

                    NICK
          Where is this going to be held?

                    MR. SPEIGEL
          Good question. Since they are
          selecting these acts from HHS, we
          will be hosting the Mr. Fahrenheit
          competition in the auditorium.
          Auditions for the show will be held
          sometime in early January.

JD scowls. Nick nudges him.

                    NICK
          Hey, JD. You should totally do it.
          You could use Autism Awareness as
          your platform.

                    JD
          Yeah, and I can defend Fairy Land
          from the Jabberwocky right after
          I'm done working the shaft.

                    MR. SPEIGEL
          I'm sorry. What was that, Mr. Dunn?

                    JD
          I said...

                    MR. SPEIGEL
          I heard what you said, young man.
          That's not appropriate. Apologize
          for that remark.

                    JD
          I'm sorry I can work the shaft.

A few audible SNICKERS escape from some of the other
students. Mr. Speigel walks up to JD.

                    MR. SPEIGEL
          Very cute.

                    JD
          You're looking dapper today, as
          well.

The SNICKERS become LAUGHS.

                    MR. SPEIGEL
          Do I look like an idiot? Am I
          really that stupid?

Mr. Speigel whips around to face the rest of the class.

                    MR. SPEIGEL
          First person to answer that reports
          to Dr. Tolini's office.

                                        CUT TO:

INT. HARTFORD HIGH SCHOOL - DR. TOLINI'S OFFICE - LATER

JD sits across from Dr. Tolini again.

                    JD
          He did ask.

                    DR. TOLINI
          JD, I know you know better than
          that. You were doing so well last
          year. Why now? Why so close to
          graduation?

                    JD
          That's nine months away.

                    DR. TOLINI
          JD...

                    JD
          It is. Just sayin'.

Dr. Tolini reads a paper from his desk.

                    DR. TOLINI
                 (in disbelief)
          I'm sorry I can work the shaft. Mm.
          I'm sorry I can work the shaft. Mm!

JD chortles. Dr. Tolini looks up at him.

                    DR. TOLINI
          Such vulgarities are unbecoming of
          a young man like yourself. I'll go
          light on you this time. Apologize
          to the class for your behavior, and
          don't do it again. Two days
          detention.

                    JD
          Damn.

                    DR. TOLINI
          Excuse me?

                    JD
          This isn't going well.

                    DR. TOLINI
          I'll say.

EXT. SENTRY RD. - AFTERNOON

JD and Amy walk up to JD's house.

                    JD
          Thanks for waiting up for me after
          detention.

                    AMY
          Sure. I just can't believe you did
          that.

                    JD
          I didn't even realize I was doing
          it. It just... sorta happened.

Jack Gladwynne exits his front door with a hedge trimmer.

                    JACK GLADWYNNE
          Oh, hey! What'cha guys think?

                    JD
          Needs more Shatner.

                    JACK GLADWYNNE
          Shatner, eh? Hmm...

He strokes his chin for a moment.

                    AMY
          When's the judging?

                    JACK GLADWYNNE
          Next week. Can't wait.

                    JD
          Awesome.

JD turns to go inside his house with a thumbs up.

                    JACK GLADWYNNE
          Hey, I got a great idea. Why don't
          you introduce Amy to your dad?

                    JD
          Because he's my dad?

                    JACK GLADWYNNE
          Jude's dad is the lead guitarist
          for Wild Billy and the Maniacs.

                    AMY
          Really? Wow! I'm a huge fan of
          theirs.

                    JACK GLADWYNNE
          Oh, I'm sure Bill won't mind
          meeting a fan. Never has before.

Amy looks at Jude with a smile that could blind the sun.

                    JD
          What?

                    AMY
          Could you introduce me to your dad?

                    JD
          Why?

                    AMY
          Because I've never met a celebrity
          before.

JD blinks at her. Amy still smiles. He blinks again.

                    AMY
          Please...

                    JD
          Fine. You win. He's in the
          basement.

                    JACK GLADWYNNE
          Don't be rude.

                    JD
          Jesus! C'mon.

JD grabs Amy by the hand and pulls her inside his house.

INT. THE DUNNS' HOUSE - BASEMENT

Bill sits at his computer station with headphones on. JD and
Amy walk down the steps. JD taps Bill's shoulder, and Bill
turns around.

                    BILL
          Oh. Hey there, Jude.

Bill notices Amy standing behind Jude.

                    BILL
          Wow. You finally brought home a
          girl. I'm so proud. My son's
          becoming a man!

Bill pretends to wipe a tear from his eye. Amy giggles while
JD glares at his father.

                    JD
          Actually, Dad... This is Jack's
          niece, Amy.

                    AMY
          Hi. It's so nice to meet you.

                    BILL
          Likewise.

Bill shakes Amy's hand. Amy almost can't contain her
excitement.

                    BILL
          So, you're Jack's niece I've been
          hearing so much about. What brings
          you guys down here today?

                    AMY
          I am such a huge fan of yours. I
          didn't know I was moving next door
          to a celebrity.

                    BILL
          I don't know if I'd call myself a
          celebrity, but I appreciate all the
          fans. You know, Jude, here, is
          shaping up to be a great musician,
          himself.

                    AMY
          Really?

                    JD
          Dad...

                    BILL
          Nonsense, Jude. You're a very
          talented keyboarder. Right now,
          we're working on guitar...

                    JD
          Which I'm still shit at.

                    BILL
          Why don't you play some keyboard
          for Amy?

                    AMY
          Yeah! That's a great idea. Are you
          gonna play in the talent show?

                    BILL
          Talent show?

                    JD
          Shut up, Amy.

JD nudges her.

                    BILL
          Tell me about this talent show.

JD rolls his eyes.

                    AMY
FME and VH1 are teaming up for a
new hit reality show. The top three
acts at the talent show make it in.

                    BILL
Whaddaya know? That's my label. I'm
sure Jude would be happy to
participate.

                    JD
Don't I get a say in this?

                    BILL
Don't tell me you don't want to do
it, now.

                    AMY
Why don't we hear a sample of what
he's capable of before he makes
that decision.

                    JD
Absolutely not!

                    BILL
Why not?

                    JD
Because I don't want to participate
in the talent show.

                    AMY
But why?

                    JD
I just don't. Okay?

                    AMY
Nope.

                    JD
What?

                    AMY
That's not an option.

                    JD
Oh?

                    AMY
Yep.

                    JD
          That's outrageous! No, I'm not
          doing it.

                    AMY
          I guess I'll just have to go to
          that upcoming RUSH concert with
          Ricky.

                    JD
          I'll do it.

                    AMY
          I thought so.

JD stomps up the stairs and slams the door behind him.

                    BILL
          Nice work. Playing the "Ricky
          Card," I see.

                    AMY
          I was just playing the RUSH card.

                    BILL
          Do you even have tickets?

Amy motions to shush him.

                    BILL
          Don't worry about it. I'll get'em.

JD returns to the basement with his 49-key synthesizer.

                    BILL
          Need some help with that, Jude?

                    JD
          I got it.

JD starts to put the synthesizer on a table on top of Bill's
paperwork.

                    BILL
          Why don't we move some of this?

Bill moves his papers out of the way, and JD sets the
synthesizer on the table. JD plugs a myriad of cables into
the synthesizer.

                    JD
          Now, I haven't played in a couple
          months, but with some practice, you
          won't even know the difference.

JD turns on the synthesizer, a black Yamaha, and fiddles with
the instrument settings for a moment.

                    JD
          Here, we go!

JD starts playing the synthesizer. Amy and Bill bob their
heads to the music. After a few bars, Bill cuts him off.

                    BILL
          All right, that was good for
          someone who hasn't played in three
          months, but it's still a little
          sloppy.

                    JD
          Bite me.

                    AMY
          You talk to your father like that?

                    JD
          I talk to everyone like that.

                    AMY
          True.

JD glares at Amy.

                    BILL
          Oh, he's just mad that I'm going on
          tour during his graduation. Don't
          take it too seriously. I don't.

                    JD
          Thanks, Dad.

                    AMY
          You know, I used to play piano back
          in Nashville.

                    BILL
          Really, now?

                    JD
          You think you can do any better?

A FEW MOMENTS LATER

Amy finishes playing on the synthesizer.

                    BILL
          That was much better technique.
          Maybe you two could play together
          in the talent show.

                    JD
          If she plays keyboard, what does
          that leave for me to play?

Bill and Amy both look at JD's guitar in the corner of the
basement studio and look back at JD.

                    JD
             What?

Bill and Amy grin.

                    JD
             What?

                                        CUT TO:

EXT. THE DUNNS' FRONT YARD - EVENING

A neighbor walks his dog past the Dunns' residence. He hears
screaming from the basement. His dog drags him away.

                    JD (O.S.)
          I'm not doing it!

                    BILL (O.S.)
          Jude, calm down! The neighbors can
          hear you.

                                        BACK TO:

INT. THE DUNNS' BASEMENT

Amy sits in a swivel desk chair, watching JD and Bill scream
at each other. She swivels toward JD.

                    JD
          You can't make me do this! I'm not
          even any good at guitar!

Amy swivels toward Bill.

                    BILL
          Can we talk about this without
          screaming?

Back to JD.

                    JD
          You wanna talk? How about we talk
          about you ditching me for a bunch
          of bandwagon fans? How about we
          talk about that?

Back to Bill.

                    BILL
          Fine. We can talk about that. Just
          stop screaming. The neighbors can
          hear all of our business.

Amy swivels back to JD. JD addresses her.

                    JD
          Can you please stop doing that;
          it's driving me up a wall!

                    BILL
          I can't talk to you at this point.
          You're too far gone.

JD clenches his fist.

                    JD
          Of course, you can't talk to me.
          You're too busy kissing Brock's...

Amy intervenes before JD can punch Bill.

                    AMY
          Hey, why don't we take a break?
          C'mon, let's go get something to
          drink.

JD reluctantly follows Amy upstairs. Amy gives Bill a quick
wink. Bill SIGHS and goes back to his computer station.

INT. THE DUNNS' HOUSE - KITCHEN - MOMENTS LATER

Amy and JD sit in the kitchen, drinking Kool-Aid.

                    AMY
          Relax. I don't think anybody wants
          anybody to get upset.

JD puts his Kool-Aid down.

                    JD
          The talent show's in six months.
          There's no way I'm going to be good
          enough for it.

                    AMY
          Not with that attitude.

                         JD
          Why do you even care, anyway? We
          just met.

                    AMY
          Because I'm a nice person, and I
          see a young man in front of me
          who's hurting inside so much, he
          can't see when other people try to
          help him.

                         JD
          I don't need any help.

                    AMY
          I guess that means you don't need
          me.

                         JD
          That's not what I said. You're
          twisting my words.

                    AMY
          Let me ask you your own question.
          Why do you care if I'm around or
          not?

                         JD
          I don't have too many friends. If I
          do this, I'll make an ass of
          myself.

                    AMY
          You have six months to change that
          outcome. For you to not make an ass
          of yourself.

                         JD
          How?

                    AMY
          By having your dad and I help you
          do the best you can.

                         JD
          He doesn't care.

Amy stares him down, putting her hand over his.

                    AMY
          He does. It's just in a different
          way than how you want him to care.
          If not for him, will you do it for
          me?

JD looks into Amy's puppy dog eyes.

                    JD
          This is hardly fair.

                    AMY
          I'm not hearing a "no."

                    JD
          Let me calm down first.

                    AMY
          Take a deep breath. Relax.

JD takes slow, deep breaths and closes his eyes.

                    AMY
          Good. We can start tomorrow if you
          want.

                    JD
          Fine.

Bill walks up the stairs.

                    BILL
          Everything all right, up here?

                    JD
          Yeah.

                    AMY
          I'll be by tomorrow. I'm holding
          you to that.

                    JD
          Whatev.

Edna walks through the back door.

                    EDNA
          Hi, guys.

Edna notices Amy.

                    EDNA
          Oh, you must be Jack's niece I've
          heard so much about.

Amy blushes.

                    AMY
          Yeah.

                    EDNA
          Would you like to stay for dinner?

                    AMY
          Oh, I don't think I...

                    EDNA
          Nonsense. You're more than welcome
          here.

                    JD
          If not for her, then will you do it
          for me?

                    AMY
          That's not even remotely fair.

                    JD
          Turnabout's fair play.

                    AMY
          Okay, I guess I can stay a little
          longer.

                    EDNA
          Great! Jude, can you and your
          father set the table?

                    JD
          Whatev.

JD turns to leave the kitchen.

                    EDNA
          Oh, and Jude?

                    JD
          Yeah?

                    EDNA
          You're grounded this weekend. Dr.
          Tolini called me at work today.

                    JD
          Damn.

                    EDNA
          No more debts to society.

                    JD
          Hooray! I'm a rich man! I don't
          have any more debts to society to
          pay! Wahoo! I'm a free man! I'm
          livin' large, tonight!

Bill and Edna look at each other. Edna's face expresses
concern, while Bill stares with a flat expression.

                    BILL
          Whatev.

INT. HARTFORD HIGH SCHOOL - MUSIC CLASS - AFTERNOON

JD and his group sit at their table while Mr. Speigel talks.
John pays close attention, sitting on the edge of his seat,
while JD stares into space and Nick rests his head on his
desk.

                    MR. SPEIGEL (O.S.)
          Blah, blah, bleep, bloop, be-doop.

John leans in closer. Mr. Speigel walks up to JD, who doesn't
flinch.

                    MR. SPEIGEL
          Blah!

JD startles and falls over backward in his chair. The class
LAUGHS.

                    JD
          Ow.

                    MR. SPEIGEL
          Try to pay more attention, Mr.
          Dunn.

Mr. Speigel turns his attention to Nick.

                    MR. SPEIGEL
          That goes for you as well, Mr.
          MacCloud.

Nick raises his hand and gives a thumbs-up.

                    MR. SPEIGEL
          Now, then. Is there anyone else who
          wishes to sign up for the talent
          competition auditions next month?

JD raises his hand. John falls forward out of his chair,
LAUGHING.

                    JOHN
          Now, that's funny.

                    MR. SPEIGEL
          Mr. Hammel, I'll thank you not to
          disrupt my class.

JD GROWLS at John.

                    JD
          Why is that funny?

                    MR. SPEIGEL
          Screw it. I'm done.

                    JOHN
          You'd be playing keys, right?

                    JD
          No, I'd be using guitar.

                    JOHN
          Dude! We'll crush you on that
          stage. Forget it. You'll never end
          up on that show.

                    JD
          Well, there are three spots on the
          show, so we can both end up on the
          show. Friendly competition, right?

                    JOHN
          Yeah, right, JD. You'll never get a
          callback. You really think they'd
          want someone who's only played for
          what? A month? Get real.

Nick picks his head up.

                    NICK
          Guys...

                    JD
          I've been playing for three months,
          ass-hole!

                    NICK
          Seriously, guys. Calm down.

                    JOHN
          Is that all? I've been playing for
          three years. What makes you so
          special, anyway?

                    NICK
               (singing)
          Imagine, there's no heaven...

                    JD
          Like, there's any actual music
          theory in your mindless shredding!

                    NICK
               (singing)
          It's easy if you try...

                    MR. SPEIGEL
          I know I can, right now.

Nick high-fives Mr. Speigel.

                    JOHN
          Why don't you learn to play without
          tabs the right way?

                    JD
          You're one to talk! Why don't you
          stop hiding behind your good buddy,
          Ricky?

                    JOHN
          I don't have to take this from an
          Aspie!

JD throws his hands in the air.

                    JD
          Oh! So, that's what this is about!
          Now, all the cards are on the
          table! Jude Dunn can't have talent
          because he's fucking autistic!

                    JOHN
          Retarded is more like it!

                    MR. SPEIGEL
          Enough! Knock it off, the both of
          you!

JD stands up.

                    JD
          I need a time out.

                    MR. SPEIGEL
          That's a wise decision, JD.

INT. HARTFORD HIGH SCHOOL - MR. D.'S CLASS - MOMENTS LATER

JD sits at a desk, drinking a bottle of water. Mr. D. sits at
an adjacent desk.

                    MR. D.
          I'm proud of the way you handled
          that, JD.

                    JD
          He just pisses me off, so much.

                    MR. D.
          Just do the best you can. People
          are going to come and go all
          throughout your life with all their
          opinions. There's only one opinion
          you'll carry around with you your
          whole life.

JD puts the water down and looks up at MR. D.

                    JD
          Mine?

                    MR. D.
          A wise man knows when to fight his
          own battles. A wiser man knows when
          not to fight.

                    JD
          But...

                    MR. D.
          Be who you are, and say how you
          feel. Because those who mind don't
          matter, and those who matter don't
          mind. Do you know who said that?

                    JD
          Dr. Seuss. But...

                    MR. D.
          Does he matter?

                    JD
          No.

                    MR. D.
          Then don't mind.

                    JD
          How will that make him stop?

                    MR. D.
          It won't.

JD raises an eyebrow.

                    MR. D.
          You can't change others; you can
          only change yourself. Set a good
          example. Be the change you want to
          see in the world.

Nick enters the room.

                    NICK
          Hey. Dude, JD. You missed all the
          drama.

                    JD
          There was more drama after I left?

                    NICK
          Yeah, man. John's dropping the
          class, which means he'll be one
          class short for graduation.

                    JD
          Which means he can't be in the
          competition, now.

                    MR. D.
          Will Mr. Speigel let him do that?

                    NICK
          He encouraged it. I told him not to
          drop it, but he flipped me off and
          quit the band.

                    JD
          Really?

                    NICK
          Yeah, and now we need a guitarist.

                    MR. D.
          Sounds like a lucky break, JD.

                    JD
          What about Asher and Brendan?

                    NICK
          I'll talk it over with them.

                    JD
          I need to talk it over with Amy,
          first.

                    NICK
          Take as long as you need.

EXT. SENTRY RD. - LATER

JD and Amy walk up to JD's house, talking. Jack Gladwynne
rakes leaves on his front lawn. The Shatner bush has a giant
see-through hole in its stomach.

                    AMY
          Yeah, sure. Do it. Serves him right
          for quitting.

                    JD
          Thanks.

Jack Gladwynne looks up at Amy and JD. JD waves.

                    JD
          Sorry about Spiffy getting into
          your bushes.

                    JACK GLADWYNNE
          Yeah, I didn't like that judge,
          anyway. That's what he got for
          getting too close to the cat in the
          Shat.

Jack Gladwynne bumps his eyebrows up and down and makes a
jazz hands motion.

                    JD
          You're losing your touch, there.

                    JACK GLADWYNNE
          Welp, I guess that didn't lighten
          the mood.

                    AMY
          What's wrong?

                    JACK GLADWYNNE
          Amy, we got a phone call from
          Nashville General Hospital this
          morning. We didn't want to upset
          you at school.

Jack Gladwynne's eyes start to tear up with a SNIFFLE.

                    JACK GLADWYNNE
          Your mother went peacefully in her
          sleep. Around 9:15, the nurse went
          to wake her up, and it was too
          late.

He starts to lose his composure.

                    JACK GLADWYNNE
          We thought we should wait to tell
          you in person.

Amy drops to her knees. JD comforts her, as she bawls on his
shoulder. JD rubs her back.

INT. HARTFORD HIGH SCHOOL - MR. D.'S CLASS - MORNING

JD and Amy sit with Mr. D., as the rest of the class file in.
Mr. D.'s hand rests on her shoulder.

Ricky enters the room.

                    RICKY
          Hey, JD. I heard you had an
          interesting music class, yesterday.

                    JD
          Not now, Ricky.

Ricky moves in closer.

                    RICKY
          Yo mama!

Amy storms out of the room.

                    JD
          I mean it, Ricky. Knock it off!

Mr. D. pulls Ricky to the side and tells him something.

A beat.

Ricky looks over at JD and puts his head down. JD glares back
for a moment and walks out after Amy.

                    RICKY
          JD, I...

                    JD (O.S.)
          Save it. Your friends are all ass-
          holes, and so are you.

INT. HARTFORD HIGH SCHOOL - MUSIC ROOM - LATER

JD works with Nick at an empty table. Sheets of paper with
musical staves printed on them are scattered across the
table. JD frowns.

                    NICK
          There's nothing anyone could have
          done.

                    JD
          Here I am, worrying about a stupid
          reality show. We can't take fame
          and fortune with us when we go, so
          what's the point of living?

                    NICK
          Nobody knows, and maybe that's the
          point.

                    JD
          What?

                    NICK
          Maybe the point's that we're
          supposed to spend our lives finding
          our purpose to answer that for
          ourselves.

                    JD
          But what's my purpose?

                    NICK
          You have to figure that out on your
          own.

JD SIGHS.

                    NICK
          Hey, man. Hakuna Matata.

                    JD
          Hmm?

                    NICK
             (singing)
          It means no worries for the rest of
          your days.

                    JD
             (singing)
          It's a problem-free philosophy.

                    NICK AND JD
                  (singing in unison)
                Hakuna Matata!

JD and Nick laugh.

                         JD
                Hey! Why don't we dedicate our
                performance in memory of Amy's mom?

                         NICK
                I like the way you think, sir. I'm
                sure Amy will really appreciate
                that.

INT. THE DUNNS' BASEMENT - EVENING

JD jams on his guitar, while Bill looks on with awe. JD
sounds much better, now.

ANGLE: JD'S FINGERS

JD's fingers flutter all over the fretboard with perfect
technique.

                         BILL
                You've been practicing for twelve
                hours today, Jude. Why don't you
                give yourself a break?

                         JD
                Can't hear you over the sound of my
                suck.

                         BILL
                You're fine. Why the sudden
                obsession?

JD stops playing.

                         JD
                I need to do this right, Dad.

                         BILL
                And you will. What you need to do
                is...

                         JD
                What I need to do is keep
                practicing.

Bill walks over to JD and puts his arm around his shoulder.

                    BILL
          Your fingers are bleeding and
          you've been practicing since you
          woke up at seven. Get some rest.

                    JD
          Just as soon as I nail this solo.

JD YAWNS.

                    BILL
          You're exhausted. You need to break
          out of this brain-lock and go to
          bed. You're not going to be able to
          help anybody if you can't function,
          yourself.

JD puts the guitar in its stand and starts to walk up the
stairs, as Edna enters the basement.

                    EDNA
          Good night, Sweetie.

                    JD
          Good night, Mom.

JD gives her a hug and walks up the stairs, closing the door
behind him.

INT. JD'S BEDROOM - MOMENTS LATER

JD lies awake in his bed with the light turned out. He looks
at his hands in the dark.

A tuxedo cat, SPIFFY, jumps on his bed and rubs up against
him. JD strokes the cat.

                    JD
          What's your purpose in life?

                    SPIFFY
          MEOW.

                    JD
          Real helpful, cat.

Spiffy lies down next to JD and PURRS.

A beat.

Bill walks up to JD's open door and KNOCKS on the doorjam.

                    BILL
          Hey, Sport.

                    JD
          Huh?

                    BILL
          Your mom and I were just talking,
          and we like that you're channelling
          all this energy into something
          productive...

                    JD
          But...

                    BILL
          We're a bit concerned about the
          amount of time you've been
          practicing each day.

                    JD
          I haven't practiced that much, have
          I?

                    BILL
          You've practiced for 80 hours out
          of the past ten days.

JD rolls over in his bed to avoid looking at Bill.

                    BILL
          Careful there, Sport. You're about
          to fall out of...

JD falls out of his bed with a THUD.

                    JD
          WHUP!

                    BILL
          Bed.

                    JD
          Ow.

Bill CHUCKLES, as JD's middle finger rises from behind the
bed, aimed at Bill. Spiffy jumps down to JD.

                    JD
          OOF! Frigging cat.

                    SPIFFY
          MEOW.

                    BILL
          Get some sleep.

JD lies on the floor until...

MORNING

Sunshine slides through the slats of JD's blinds. Spiffy
sleeps on JD's face on the floor.

The cat perks up and runs out of the room in a hurry.

                    JD
          Frigging cat.

                         SPIFFY (O.S.)
          MEOW.

JD sits up, rubbing and cracking his neck. He picks himself
up and heads for...

THE KITCHEN

Bill and Edna sit at the kitchen table, eating.

Bill reads a newspaper, as Edna sips her coffee.

                    BILL
          Mornin'.

                    JD
          Yes. It is morning.

                    EDNA
          Something wrong?

                    JD
          I slept on the floor with a cat on
          my face last night?

                    BILL
          You have any schoolwork for Monday?

                    JD
          No.

                    BILL
          Good. Eat some breakfast.

                    JD
          I don't even like bacon.

Bill pauses with a strip of bacon hanging out of his mouth.
CRUNCH.

                    BILL
          Whose son are you? Don't like
          bacon...

                    EDNA
          What's on your schedule for today?

                    JD
          Band practice at 2:30.

                    EDNA
          Don't you think you're working a
          little too hard?

                    JD
          I'll be fine. We're dedicating our
          performance to Amy's mom.

                    EDNA
          Oh, that's nice.

                    BILL
          Are you going to be able to handle
          it if you don't get picked?

                    JD
          Oh, we're getting picked. The Nitro
          Pumpkins will be on that show.

                    BILL
          If you say so.

INT. NICK'S GARAGE - EVENING

The NITRO PUMPKINS practice in the garage, with the door
open. The garage is empty, save for the band and their
equipment.

There's a beautiful sunset tonight, not that anybody notices.

ANGLE: ASHER PLAYS BASS GUITAR.

ANGLE: BRENDAN FLAILS WILDLY ON THE DRUMS.

Nick stops playing his keyboard and motions for everybody to
stop.

Brendan continues flailing.

                         NICK
          Okay, Brendan. The drums work.

Nick grabs the drumsticks from Brendan.

                         NICK
          Can we be a tad more serious?

A beat.

                         ASHER
          It's 8:42. Maybe we should call it
          a night.

                         JD
          Already? I was just getting
          started.

                         NICK
          I like the enthusiasm, but we're
          all exhausted, dude.

                         JD
          You are.

                         BRENDAN
          What's with all the seriousness,
          anyway?

                         NICK
          Yeah, man. What's up?

                         JD
          I just wanna do this right. We are
          dedicating it and all.

Nick smirks.

                         NICK
          You like her, don't you?

                         JD
          What? Who?

                         NICK
          You know who I mean.

Nick's smirk becomes an impish grin.

                         NICK
          You like Amy. That's why you're
          pushing yourself so hard.

                    JD
          Not here; not now, Nick.

                    NICK
          Hey, it's noble. Just remember to
          take care of yourself, too.

                    BRENDAN
          This isn't another thing like with
          Lauren Snyder, is it?

                    JD
          You tryin' to say something, big
          guy?

                    ASHER
          Whoa! Chill out. He's not trying to
          say anything.

                    JD
          But he just said...

                    ASHER
          Be the bigger man. Don't let anyone
          get to you. Just let it go. Are you
          the bigger man?

                    JD
          I'd like to think so.

                    ASHER
          Then don't worry about it.

                    NICK
          C'mon, Jude. Let's take a walk.

EXT. NICK'S NEIGHBORHOOD - LATER

The sun has finished setting. JD and Nick walk with their
winter coats on.

                    NICK
          I didn't mean to start something,
          back there.

                    JD
          That's okay. To tell you the truth,
          I'm exhausted, too.

                    NICK
          Just remember what we talked about
          in the music room.

                    JD
          What?

                    NICK
               (singing)
          Hakuna Matata.

                    NICK AND JD
               (chanting in unison)
          Hakuna! Matata! Hakuna! Matata!

Nick and JD nudge each other and laugh.

INT. HARTFORD HIGH SCHOOL - AUDITORIUM - AFTERNOON

The Nitro Pumpkins perform a sound check on stage, fiddling
with different knobs and plugging in cables.

BROCK TRENT, 42, sits a few rows back in the audience. His
hair has a gray racing stripe on one side. A few other people
sit with him, holding clipboards.

A myriad of roadies and cameramen adjust sound settings and
lighting.

Amy watches from a distance, backstage. Ricky approaches her.

                    RICKY
          I'm sorry I said that thing. I
          didn't know.

                    AMY
          Why do you hate Jude, so much?

                    RICKY
          It's not that I hate Jude so much
          as he makes it so easy. Like a
          walking bull's eye.

                    AMY
          But why? Why even go out of your
          way to bug him?

                    RICKY
          I... I just... I dunno.

Amy stares him down.

                    RICKY
          It's just that when we were kids,
          everybody did it. I guess it just
          kinda... stuck.

                    AMY
          Just because someone else does
          something, doesn't mean you should.

                    RICKY
          I'll take that into consideration.

Ricky starts to walk away, but stops a moment.

                    RICKY
          Tell him I said, "good luck."

                    AMY
          I'll let him know.

Ricky walks off down...

THE HALLWAY

Mr. D. exits the main office and bumps into Ricky.

                    MR. D.
          Hey, there.

                    RICKY
          Mr. D.?

                    MR. D.
          Something wrong?

                    RICKY
          I feel like I don't even know
          myself, anymore.

                    MR. D.
          Wanna talk about it?

                    RICKY
          I've been a horrible person.

                    MR. D.
          There are no horrible people. Their
          actions may be horrible, but
          there's no such thing as a horrible
          person.

                    RICKY
          No, I think my actions speak louder
          than words.

                    MR. D.
     I'm not gonna lie, Ricky. Your
     actions toward JD have been
     deplorable and despicable.

Ricky looks at his feet.

                    MR. D.
     But. We are more than just our
     actions. We make choices. We always
     have the option to make new
     choices. We can always change our
     actions in the future.

                    RICKY
     So, what do I do, now?

                    MR. D.
     That, Mr. Mallo, is up to you. I
     have to get to a meeting. Let me
     know if you need to talk about
     anything else.

Mr. D. turns to walk down the hallway.

                    MR. D.
              (singing)
     ...As we wind on down the road, our
     shadows taller than our souls.
     There walks a lady we all know, who
     shines white light and wants to
     show how everything still turns to
     gold. And if you listen very hard,
     the tune will come to you at last.

His words echo throughout the hallway.

                    RICKY
              (singing to himself)
     When we all are one and one is
     all...
              (spoken)
     To be a rock and not to roll.

Ricky turns his head to look back at the auditorium.

Amy still stands at the backstage door, watching.

                    RICKY
              (singing)
     ...And she's buying a stairway to
     heaven.

AUDITORIUM - MOMENTS LATER

MONTAGE:

The Nitro Pumpkins perform their audition song, a cover of "Carry On Wayward Son."

Jude's fingers fly up and down the frets, playing each note with passion.

Brendan keeps the beat on the drums along with Asher on bass.

Nick sings and plays keyboard at the same time.

The judges scribble in their clipboards.

Brock bobs his head to the beat and taps his foot.

Amy claps along.

Ricky sits outside on a step with his face buried in his hands.

The Nitro Pumpkins finish their performance.

Brock stands up and claps.

                    BROCK
          I wouldn't expect anything less
          from Wild Billy's son. That was
          studio quality, right there. What's
          your platform?

                    NICK
          Autism Awareness. JD, here, is an
          Aspie.

                    BROCK
          I know. I work with his father.

                    JD
          Don't I know it.

                    BROCK
          Do you even know who I am?

                    JD
          You're Brock Trent. You're the guy
          who told my dad he can't attend my
          graduation in June.

                    BROCK
          I did? That would be a crime.
          Anyone who plays like that deserves
          to have his father attend his
          graduation.

                    JD
          So...

                    BROCK
          I'll see what I can work out. See
          you guys in March.

                    NICK
          Wait, you mean...

                    JUDGE #1
          You're in.

                    JUDGE #2
          Congratulations! You'll be
          receiving further instructions at
          the next meeting in February.

The Nitro Pumpkins CHEER.

JD double high-fives Nick. Asher pumps his fist in the air.

                    ASHER
          Woo-hoo!

Brendan crashes on the drums.

                    BRENDAN
          Animal!

Brock smiles.

EXT. SENTRY RD. - LATER

JD walks Amy home.

                    AMY
          That was amazing. I'm so proud of
          you.

                    JD
          Wait until Dad finds out. He won't
          believe it! I mean, I hardly
          believe it.

They reach JD's house. Jack Gladwynne shovels snow off his
sidewalk. He looks up and waves at JD and Amy.

                    JACK GLADWYNNE
          Hey, guys! How'd it go?

                    JD
          We're in!

                    JACK GLADWYNNE
          Fantastic! I can't wait to see the
          competition. How many bands got in?

                    AMY
          Five.

                    JACK GLADWYNNE
          Out of how many?

                    JD
          Fourteen.

                    JACK GLADWYNNE
          Outstanding!

Bill storms out the front door, a portable phone in his hand
and a scowl on his face.

                    BILL
          Jude! What did you do? My tour got
          pushed back a month.

                    AMY
          JD didn't do anything. Brock was
          there, and...

                    BILL
          Oh, no! Tell me you didn't...

                    JD
          I didn't.

                    BILL
          Don't lie to me, Jude.

                    JD
          But I really didn't. He saw me play
          and said it was a crime to make you
          miss my graduation.

                    BILL
          How'd it come up?

                    JD
          He asked if I knew who he was?

                    BILL
          What did you say?

                    JD
          I told him about the situation,
          and...

                    BILL
          Jude...

                    JD
          Now we both get what we want.

                    BILL
          That's not the point, son.

Bill SIGHS.

                    BILL
          I was counting on that revenue to
          get you your graduation gift. Now I
          have to figure everything out all
          over again.

A beat.

                    BILL
          Did you at least get in the talent
          competition?

                    JD
          Along with four other bands.

                    BILL
          Congrats!

Bill gives Jude a big hug.

                    JD
          Dad...

                    BILL
          I am so proud of you.

                    JD
          Dad, I have to pee.

Jack Gladwynne laughs. Amy face-palms. Bill lets go.

                    BILL
          You really know how to kill the
          moment, don't you? I'll let you
          tell your mother the good news.

JD disappears inside, leaving the front door open.

                    BILL
          Amy, do us all a favor?

                    AMY
          Yeah?

                    BILL
          Make sure he doesn't overwork
          himself?

                    AMY
          On it.

                    BILL
          Thanks.

Spiffy jumps out the front door and plays in the snow piles.
He inadvertently destroys a snowman and knocks over Bill's
ice sculpture at the curb.

                    BILL
          Frigging cat.

                    SPIFFY
          MEOW.

Jack and Amy burst out laughing. Bill GRUNTS and chases the
cat.

INT. THE DUNNS' LIVING ROOM - MOMENTS LATER

JD sits on the couch, watching *VH1's Behind the Music*.

LOUD RUMBLING can be heard from outside the house.

                    BILL (O.S.)
          Ow!

A pair of hands stretch from behind the door, throwing Spiffy
inside the house.

                    SPIFFY
          RWOWR!

The door slams shut, and the cat runs up the stairs.

                    JD
          Good cat.

INT. BROCK TRENT'S OFFICE - MORNING

Brock's office is akin to the mythical "corner office," with
a large window, two couches, a large, flat-screen TV, and his
Mahogany desk.

Brock sits behind his desk on the phone.

                    BROCK
          I think it's a great idea... Yes, I
          saw him play... Phenomenal... I
          want to get him a contract... Win
          or lose, he still deserves
          something for his effort... Four
          months ago, he didn't even know how
          to play one... I'll get right on
          that. Thank you... Bye, bye.

Brock hangs up the phone. He pulls out a folder and writes on
it.

ANGLE: THE FOLDER: NITRO PUMPKINS

Brock puts the folder in his desk drawer and pokes his head
out his glass office door.

                    BROCK
          Hey, Cammi! I need you to cancel my
          12 o'clock. I have to work on a new
          deal coming up.

INT. HARTFORD HIGH SCHOOL - CAFETERIA - AFTERNOON

Amy and the members of the Nitro Pumpkins chat at the lunch
table.

JD's the only member of the group still eating a meatball
sub.

                    JD
          Oh my God, this is good.

                    AMY
          I don't think I've ever seen you
          savor your food before.

JD gulps down the remainder of a meatball.

                    JD
          Huh?

                    NICK
          Yeah, you usually finish first.

                    JOHN (O.S.)
          That's what she said.

JD puts his sub down and turns around to face John. John
stands behind him with his arms crossed.

                    JD
          Hello, John. To what do I owe this
          honor?

                    JOHN
          I'll never understand how an Ass-
          burger like you got into the talent
          show. My money's on the Buzz Fuzz.

                    AMY
          Ew. You're rooting for Randy Buzz?

                    JOHN
          He's better than the retard, over
          here.

John motions to JD. JD stares him in the eye with a vacant
expression.

                    JOHN
          Cat got yer tongue?

                    JD
          Don't get me wrong; I'm absolutely
          livid. We're so far beyond livid
          that the U.S. Military wouldn't be
          enough to save you if I lost my
          temper right now.

                    JOHN
          Is that a threat?

                    JD
          No, just a fact. Nothing I say or
          do is going to change your
          behavior.

John CHORTLES.

                    JOHN
          Dork.

                    NICK
          You're the only dork, here, John.

                    JOHN
          What're you even doing with a loser
          like Dunn, anyway?

                    JD
          Weren't you the one who quit his
          band and dropped a class during a
          temper tantrum?

                    JOHN
          Shows how much you know! The only
          reason you got in was because of
          your loser dad.

JD stands up and gets in John's face.

                    JD
          My father is more of a man than
          you'll ever be.

                    JOHN
          Is that so?

                    AMY
          Knock it off, John.

                    JOHN
          Then why isn't he signed to a
          bigger label? I'll tell you why.
          It's because everyone knows his
          music sucks.

ANGLE: RICKY WATCHES FROM A COUPLE TABLES OVER.

                    AMY
          Go do something else, creep!

                    JOHN
          What'cha gonna do about it? Hit me
          like a girl?

                    NICK
          John...

                    JD
          No, I'm going to walk away.

                    JOHN
          Coward.

JD turns and walks away.

                    JOHN
          What? You're just going to run?
          Fight like a man, wuss!

JD stops.

Mr. D. Walks into the cafeteria, pausing to watch JD's reaction.

                    JD
          A wise man knows when to fight his
          own battles. A wiser man knows when
          not to fight.

JD walks away.

Mr. D. smiles and walks out.

                    JOHN
          Pussy!

                    JD
          Meow.

JD exits the cafeteria. The lunch bell rings.

HARTFORD HIGH SCHOOL - HALLWAY - MOMENTS LATER

John walks along the crowded hallway. Ricky comes up behind him.

                    RICKY
          Hey, bud. Can I talk to you a sec?

Ricky pushes John into...

THE MEN'S ROOM

The men's room is empty except for John and Ricky.

                    JOHN
          Dude! What the hell?

Ricky punches John in the face with a CRACK.

John falls to the ground.

                    RICKY
          What the hell was that in the
          cafeteria? Are you really that much
          of a jack-hole?

                    JOHN
          I'm the jack-hole? Take a look at
          the retard. He wouldn't even fight
          me.

Ricky grabs John by the collar.

                    RICKY
          He's smarter than you are.

Ricky punches him three more times. John falls backward
against a urinal.

                    JOHN
          Since when are you all buddy-buddy
          with him?

                    RICKY
          Since I stopped being an ass-hole
          like you!

A beat.

                    RICKY
          Tell on me if you want. I don't
          care. Everyone will know why I did
          it.

Ricky leaves the men's room.

Mr. D. walks out from a bathroom stall with a FLUSH.

                    MR. D.
          That could've gone better.

                    JOHN
          Did you see what he did?

                    MR. D.
          No, but I saw what you did to JD.

                    JOHN
          He had it coming.

                    MR. D.
          So did you.

                    JOHN
          Hey!

                    MR. D.
          I see before me a waste of energy,
          attacking those he feels threatened
          by.

                    JOHN
          Threatened?

                    MR. D.
          He's found his niche. I suggest you
          think long and hard about finding
          yours.

A beat.

                    MR. D.
          Shouldn't you get to class, or
          something?

                    JOHN
          I have study hall.

                    MR. D.
          You also have three days detention
          with me. Do you need a nurse?

                    JOHN
          I'm fine.

A drop of blood streams down from John's nose.

                    MR. D.
          Let's get you to the nurse.

EXT. HARTFORD HIGH SCHOOL - LATER

Ricky passes by the parking lot just as Mr. D. unlocks his
car.

                    MR. D.
          Mr. Mallo. That was a nice gesture
          you made in the men's room, today.
          Although, I don't necessarily
          approve of your methods.

                    RICKY
          You saw?

                    MR. D.
          No, but I heard everything.

                    RICKY
          I can explain...

                    MR. D.
          I'm sure you can. Detention with me
          tomorrow.

                    RICKY
          That's all?

                    MR. D.
You have one thing in your favor.

                    RICKY
What's that?

                    MR. D.
You did the right thing, standing
up for JD. Next time, tone down the
violence.

Ricky smiles.

                    RICKY
Okay.

A beat.

                    RICKY
Do you have time to talk about
something?

                    MR. D.
Like what?

                    RICKY
I thought about what you said that
time. About the choices that we
make.

                    MR. D.
And?

                    RICKY
What if I make things worse?

                    MR. D.
That's a risk we all have to take.
Otherwise, what's the point of
living if we're not going to do
what it takes to live?

                    RICKY
How do I know I'm making the right
choices?

                    MR. D.
You'll know it when the time's
right.

                    RICKY
When's that?

                    MR. D.
          That, Mr. Mallo, I don't have an
          answer for. The world works in
          mysterious ways.

Ricky and Mr. D. stare at each other for a beat.

                    RICKY
          Thanks.

                    MR. D.
          No problem. That's what I'm here
          for.

Mr. D. gets into his car, and turns on the engine. The radio
blasts "Friends in Low Places" by Garth Brooks.

Ricky watches Mr. D. peel away in a red Mazda.

A beat.

Ricky SIGHS and walks away.

                    RICKY
               (singing)
          I've got friends in low places...

EXT. SENTRY RD. - MOMENTS LATER

JD and Amy walk up to JD's house. Ricky stands in the
driveway with his arms crossed.

                    JD
          Ricky? What are you doing here?

                    RICKY
          I saw what happened at lunch.

                    AMY
          Then you know what a big jerk he
          was.

                    RICKY
          I just wanted to apologize for
          John's behavior.

                    JD
          Okay...

                    RICKY
          No, really. I also wanted to
          apologize for the way I've treated
          you all these years.

                    I've made some poor decisions in
                    the past, and I know I can't
                    correct all of them, but I have to
                    at least try.

                              JD
                    How do I know I can trust you?
                    That's not something that can be
                    repaired so easily.

                              RICKY
                    Then trust this. I want to make it
                    up to you.

Amy looks back and forth at Ricky and JD.

                              AMY
                    Where's all this coming from?

                              RICKY
                    I... I've been doing some thinking
                    lately.

                              JD
                    You want to rebuild my trust? Get
                    to know me.

JD extends his hand.

A beat.

Ricky takes it, and they both shake on it.

                              JD
                    You wanna come in?

                              RICKY
                    Naw, I gotta get home. My little
                    sister's got her first grade play
                    tonight.

                              JD
                    Oh, cool!

                              RICKY
                    Yeah. Good luck with the talent
                    competition.

                              JD
                    Thank you.

Ricky walks off into the distance.

Bill walks out the front door.

                    BILL
          Was that Ricky Mallo?

                    JD
          Yup.

                    BILL
          You got mail. It's on the table in
          the kitchen.

                    JD
          Thanks.

JD enters the house.

                    AMY
          Something wrong?

                    BILL
          The last time Ricky came over, they
          got into a huge fight. Something
          about popularity. I don't
          necessarily remember what started
          it.

                    AMY
          I wonder if they even remember.

ANGLE: RICKY ROUNDS THE CORNER IN THE DISTANCE.

                    BILL
          I'm not entirely sure they do.
          You're always welcome to come in;
          you know that.

                    AMY
          I have some homework to do.

                    BILL
          You better get to it, then.

Bill turns around and goes inside.

Amy pauses a beat, then leaves.

INT. THE DUNNS' LIVING ROOM

Bill finds JD sitting on the couch, reading a letter.

                    JD
          Hey, Dad! It says I got into UCLA!

                    BILL
          That's wonderful.

                    JD
          You don't sound too excited.

                    BILL
          Everything go okay at school today?

                    JD
          For the most part.

                    BILL
          You know you can always come to me
          if you wanna talk.

                    JD
          Thanks.

                    BILL
          I gotta get back to work in the
          studio.

Bill walks out of the room.

JD reaches to open another letter.

                    JD
          Hmm... This one's from UArts.

INT. THE DUNNS' BASEMENT - EVENING

Bill sits at his recording station on his portable phone.

                    BILL
          Listen, I know sales are slowing
          down... Yes, I understand that...
          Look, I know we need a new album
          release this summer, and I'm
          trying... Brock, listen to me...
          Yes, I know it's been two years
          since... Just give me until that
          tour... I promise we can turn this
          around. Just give me a chance to do
          it!

JD walks down the basement steps.

                    JD (O.S.)
          Dad?

                    BILL
          Can I call you back? My son just
          walked in... Yeah, I'll consider
          it. Thanks... Buh-bye.

Bill hangs up the phone.

                    BILL
          What's up, Sports Fan?

JD sits down next to Bill.

                    JD
          Something did happen in the
          cafeteria today.

                    BILL
          You didn't get into any...

                    JD
          No. No, I'm not in any trouble, but
          somebody said that you're a loser
          because you're not on a bigger
          record label.

                    BILL
          ...And it bothered you.

                    JD
          I know your last album didn't make
          it too far up the Top 100 lists,
          but your next one should be better,
          right?

Bill puts his arm around JD's shoulder.

                    BILL
          Jude... Don't worry about me. You
          just focus on what you're doing.
          Brock thinks you've got potential,
          so let's not let him down.

                    JD
          You need a miracle, don't you?

                    BILL
          No! No. We're fine, Jude. Just
          concentrate on your band.

                    JD
          Wow, that biblical, huh?

                    BILL
          Jude! Listen to me. You're focused
          right now. Put that energy into
          your life. I promise things will
          turn out for the better, 'kay?

                    JD
          I thought about what you said
          earlier. About needing the money
          for my gift. Are we in trouble?

                    BILL
          No, Jude. That's something for your
          mom and I to worry about. You just
          get through 12th grade. All right?

JD looks up at Bill.

                    JD
          Okay.

JD gets up and walks up the stairs.

A beat.

Bill picks the phone up off his desk and throws it across the
room.

                    BILL
          Fuck!

He bangs his fists on the desk.

                    BILL
          Fuck! Fuck! Fuck!

Edna runs down the stairs.

                    EDNA
          Bill? Are you okay, Honey?

Bill rests his head on the desk, as Edna rubs his shoulders.

JD watches from the steps, unnoticed.

                                        DISSOLVE TO:

INT. THE DUNNS' HOUSE - KITCHEN - AFTERNOON

JD stands with the fridge door wide open. He pulls out a
pitcher of a red liquid.

                    JD
               (singing)
          Kool-Aid, yeah!

               EDNA (O.S.)
          I'm home! Jude, can you help me
          carry some stuff in?

                    JD
          Dammit. Yeah, Mom!

JD puts down his pitcher of Kool-Aid and walks out of the
kitchen. He returns moments later.

                    JD
          No! No! I'm not doing it! No!

Edna follows him into the kitchen.

                    EDNA
          She's your sister, and she's
          staying with us this semester.

                    JD
          Then I'm moving out!

BERNADETTE, 21, with shoulder-length brown hair and JD's
height walks into the kitchen.

                    BERNADETTE
          So nice to see you, too.

                    JD
          Get out!

                    BERNADETTE
          I did. Now I'm back.

                    JD
          Then I'm getting out.

Edna blocks JD from reaching the doorway into the dining
room.

                    EDNA
          Both of you be nice. You're family.

                    JD
          Only by blood.

                    BERNADETTE
          Now, why would my favorite baby
          brother say that?

                    JD
          Because you're a...

                         EDNA
               Jude! Stop it!

                    JD
          Now hang on! She disappears for
          four years, doesn't come home for
          birthdays and holidays, and she's
          supposed to be family?

                         BERNADETTE
               Hey, we kept you, didn't we?

                    JD
          Bitch!

                         BERNADETTE
               Real original...

JD grabs the pitcher of Kool-Aid and splashes it at
Bernadette.

Bernadette dodges, and the Kool-Aid hits Bill in the face, as
he opens the door to the basement studio.

                    JD
          Oh, shit.

                         BILL
               The funny part is, I was coming up
               for something to drink.

                         EDNA
               Are you all right, Bill?

                         BILL
               Peachy.

                    JD
          Actually, it was fruit punch.

                         BILL
               Go help your sister bring her
               things in. If you don't, you can
               kiss the talent show good-bye.

                    JD
          On it.

JD disappears from the kitchen.

                    BERNADETTE
          You did tell him I was coming,
          didn't you?

                    EDNA
          Not exactly. No.

                    BERNADETTE
          That explains it.

                    BILL
          Go tell your brother where you want
          everything.

                    BERNADETTE
          My room still exists, right?

                    EDNA
          Just do what your father says,
          okay, Bernie?

Bernadette disappears from the kitchen.

                    BILL
          Can you hand me a paper towel?

INT. THE DUNN'S HOUSE - BERNADETTE'S ROOM

The walls are painted purple with red carpeting. Her bed is a
disaster area; her bed is unmade and the sheets lie wherever
they fell. Old magazines are strewn across the floor. Just
how she left it.

Bernadette walks into the room and points at the bed. JD
follows behind her with three suitcases.

                    BERNADETTE
          You can just put those on the bed.

JD drops the suitcases on the floor where he stands and walks
out.

                    BERNADETTE
          Danke.

                    JD (O.S.)
          Bitte.

INT. HARTFORD HIGH SCHOOL - CAFETERIA - AFTERNOON

JD sits at the table with Amy and his bandmates. JD eats
feverishly, as if taking his anger out on the food. The
others sit and stare in amazement.

                    AMY
          Wait a minute! You have a sister?
          You never mentioned her before.

                    NICK
          Oh, yeah! The two of them have been
          going at it for years now. I didn't
          think she was ever coming back, JD.

Ricky walks up to the table with two plates of cake.

                    RICKY
          Here's that cake you wanted.

Ricky hands JD a plate of cake and sits down.

JD takes the fork and stabs the cake repeatedly.

                    JD
          Die, bitch! Die! Die! Die!

Ricky shoots a concerned glance to Amy.

                    AMY
          His sister's back.

                    RICKY
          Wow. I didn't think she was ever
          coming back. Especially since the
          graduation incident.

                    AMY
          Excuse me, but...

A beat.

                    AMY
          Did you say graduation incident?

                    NICK
          Yeah, Bernadette didn't invite Jude
          to her graduation party. JD, here,
          got sent out with his cousin to the
          zoo.

JD looks up at Nick and glares.

                    JD
Bitch tried to push me in with the
monkeys.

                    AMY
I'm sorry, but maybe I'd be a bit
more sympathetic if I had known you
had a sister.

                    JD
You're not missing much.

                    RICKY
You really aren't.

                    JD
She never called, wrote, visited,
or anything in the past four years.
Now, all of a sudden, she's
commuting from home.

                    AMY
I feel like I'm missing part of the
story. What was she like when she
was home?

                    JD
Again. You're not missing much.

                    AMY
Jude! She's your sister. I feel
like you should have some special
place for her in your life.

                    JD
Yeah. Under my foot.

                    AMY
Jude!

                    JD
She's a bitch!

                    AMY
She's your sister!

                    JD
Only by blood.

                    AMY
Am I the only one who didn't know
about this?

                    JD
          Nobody told me she was coming back,
          either.

                    AMY
          Cute, Jude.

                    JD
          What?

                    AMY
          Nothing. Never mind.

Amy stands up and walks away.

                    JD
          Was it something I said?

                    RICKY
          You're a special kind of special,
          aren't you?

                    JD
          What?

                    NICK
          Nothing. Just eat your food and
          calm down.

JD shrugs and stabs the cake again before eating it.

INT. HARTFORD HIGH SCHOOL - HALLWAY - LATER

Amy storms through the hallway toward Mr. D.'s classroom.
Ricky runs up behind her.

                    RICKY
          Amy! Hold up!

Amy stops and turns around.

                    AMY
          You know, you haven't been my
          favorite person, either.

                    RICKY
          I know. Just hear me out. JD... He
          doesn't really pick up on things
          like you and I do.

                    AMY
          Really, now? I wouldn't have
          guessed.

                    RICKY
          Yes, well...

Amy grabs Ricky and cries into his shoulder.

                    AMY
          I lost a family member recently,
          and JD doesn't even care about his
          own family.

Ricky rubs her back.

                    RICKY
          They had a tense relationship.

                    AMY
          My mother died, Ricky. I'm all
          alone except for my aunt and uncle.
          I need someone who can pick up on
          what a living hell my life is,
          right now.

Ricky and Amy share a kiss.

                    RICKY
          I... I'm sorry. That won't happen
          again...

                    AMY
          No, no. It's okay.

Amy wipes tears from her face.

                    AMY
          I kinda liked it.

                    RICKY
          I thought you and...

                    AMY
          Oh, no. We're just friends.

JD walks up to Amy and Ricky.

                    JD
          What did I say that has you all
          bent out of shape?

                    RICKY
          JD...

                    JD
          No, hold on a minute! She's just my
          sister! It's not like she really
          matters in my life.

                    RICKY
          Um...

Amy whips around with a left hook.

                                        SMASH CUT TO:

EXT. SENTRY RD. - LATER

Jack Gladwynne shovels snow from his sidewalk. Amy walks up
alone.

                    JACK GLADWYNNE
          What? No Jude, today?

                    AMY
          He had an early dismissal.

                    JACK GLADWYNNE
          What happened?

                    AMY
          I punched him in the face in Mr.
          D.'s class. With any luck, I gave
          him a concussion.

                    JACK GLADWYNNE
          Amy! Come now, you two are such
          good friends.

                    AMY
          Were such good friends.

                    JACK GLADWYNNE
          What happened?

                    AMY
          I found out he had a sister, and he
          doesn't even care about the fact
          that I just lost Mom.

                    JACK GLADWYNNE
          Yes, but...

                    AMY
          He's just a callous jack-ass.

                    JACK GLADWYNNE
          It has nothing to do with that. I
          can assure you. Bernie and Jude
          never got along. Then again, what
          siblings do?

                    AMY
          That's still no reason to act like
          a jerk-off about it.

                    JACK GLADWYNNE
          She's been a negative force in his
          life for a long time. I'm sure
          things will quiet down soon.

                    AMY
          They better quiet down soon. I just
          might have to kill him if they
          don't.

                    JACK GLADWYNNE
          Amy... The thing you have to
          remember is that Jude's not most
          cases. Why don't you go apologize
          to him.

A beat.

                    AMY
     Fine.

Jack goes back to shoveling while Amy walks up to...

THE DUNNS' HOUSE - FRONT DOOR

Amy knocks on the door. Bernadette answers.

                    BERNADETTE
          You must be the girl who clocked my
          brother.

                    AMY
          You must be the sister he doesn't
          even care about.

                    BERNADETTE
          He's a jerk, but only I get to hit
          him like that.

                    AMY
          Why are you so mean to him?

                    BERNADETTE
          Hey, you punched him.

                    AMY
          I wanted to apologize to him for
          that.

                    BERNADETTE
          And I wanted to not have to pick up
          my brother from school today. That
          didn't happen.

                    AMY
          Can I apologize to him?

                    BERNADETTE
          Nope.

                    JD (O.S.)
          Hey, Bernie! Who is it?

                    BERNADETTE
               (calling back)
          Nobody, go back to sleep.

Bernadette turns back to Amy.

                    BERNADETTE
          You need to leave.

Amy walks away, and Bernadette slams the door shut.

INT. HARTFORD HIGH SCHOOL - MR. D.'S CLASS - MORNING

JD and Amy sit opposite each other, as Mr. D. sits between
them.

                    MR. D.
          You two have been good friends all
          year. Now, you seem to hate each
          other. I want to know why.

                    AMY
          I got mad because my mother died a
          while back, and here he is not
          caring about any of his family.

                    MR. D.
          So you punched him.

                    AMY
          Yes. I tried to apologize, but...

                    JD
          When? When did you try to
          apologize? No visits, no phone
          calls, nothing!

                    AMY
          Your sister answered the door!

                    JD
          Where was I?

                    AMY
          Apparently asleep.

JD's expression becomes vacant for a moment.

DIAL-UP NOISES can be heard, while JD computes Amy's story.

A MACINTOSH START-UP SOUND rings in his head, as his eyes
widen.

                    JD
          I'm gonna kill the bitch!

                    MR. D.
          Jude! Unnecessary language. Stay
          calm. Amy, is there anything you'd
          like to say, right now.

                    AMY
          I'm sorry, Jude. I let my anger
          control me, and I punched you. I
          set a bad example for you, and I
          hope you can forgive me.

                    MR. D.
          Jude?

                    JD
          What do you mean you're setting a
          bad example for me? I'm 18, not
          three!

                    MR. D.
          You know that isn't what she meant.
          Do you accept her apology?

                    JD
          Does she understand why I hate my
          sister now?

                    MR. D.
          That's not a condition of
          acceptance.

                    AMY
          No, wait. I'll answer that. I
          understand you hate your sister. A
          lot of siblings hate each other. At
          the end of the day, you two are
          still family. Instead of making
          life worse for each other, try
          making it better.

                    JD
          Tell her that.

Mr. D. begins scribbling notes on a clipboard.

                    AMY
          I'm going to tell both of you that.
          You need to meet her halfway, too.

A beat.

                    AMY
          Don't let her ruin your friendship.
          Okay?

Amy puts her hand out. Jude shakes it.

                    JD
          Fine.

                    MR. D.
          Good. You guys can go to your first
          block classes, now. I'll see you
          after school, Ms. Gladwynne. You
          still have a detention to serve.

                    AMY
          Right.

INT. THE DUNNS' LIVING ROOM - AFTERNOON

JD walks through the front door to find the room empty and
the TV on. He flips the channel to an episode of Dragonball
GT and sits down on the couch.

Bernadette walks in with a glass of Kool-Aid.

                    BERNADETTE
          Hey! I was watching that!

                    JD
          Is that my Kool-Aid?

                    BERNADETTE
          It belongs to the family.

                    JD
          Funny thing happened in school
          today. Amy said you slammed the
          door in her face when she came over
          to apologize.

                    BERNADETTE
          Yeah, so? You don't need a witch
          like her.

                    JD
          I don't need a witch like you
          telling me which witch I need.

JD tilts his head for a moment.

                    JD
          Yeah, I think that made sense...

                    BERNADETTE
          She hit you.

                    JD
          That's a love tap compared to the
          zoo incident.

                    BERNADETTE
          We talked about this, Jude. We
          couldn't risk a blowout at my
          party.

                    JD
          I'm your brother. Didn't that
          thought cross your mind?

                    BERNADETTE
          Yes. Of course, it did.

                    JD
          The monkey Frenched me! You never
          even apologized for it!

                    BERNADETTE
          Hey, I didn't push you over the
          fence!

Edna opens the front door.

                    JD
          You're the one who requested I be
          there.

                    Nobody discussed anything with me
                    back then, and nobody discusses
                    anything with me now.

Bernadette motions their mother to leave the house.

                         JD
                    What? What're you doing now?

JD whips around and sees only Edna.

                         JD
                    What's going on, this time?

                         EDNA
               Nothing.

A dog BARKS off-screen.

                         JD
                    Tell me you didn't...

                         EDNA
               Okay, we didn't.

                         BERNADETTE
               To be fair, this was all my idea.

                         JD
               I have a cat!

                         BERNADETTE
               His name's Scooby, and he's super
               sweet with cats and small children.

                         SCOOBY (O.S.)
               WOOF!

                         BERNADETTE
               What could go wrong?

Spiffy walks by the front door. His fur spikes up. He hisses
and runs back up the steps.

                         BILL (O.S.)
               Whoa!

SCOOBY, 8 weeks, a Great Dane puppy twice the size of Spiffy,
runs up the steps after the cat with his leash trailing
behind him.

                         SCOOBY
               WOOF! WOOF! WOOF! WOOF! WOOF!

                    JD
          Does that answer your question?

                    BERNADETTE
          We were going to surprise you.

                    JD
          You're just full of surprises,
          aren't you?

                    BERNADETTE
          I'm trying to make it up to you.

                    JD
          By sacrificing my cat to the gods
          of Scooby Doo?

                    BERNADETTE
          Hey! You can name him Scooby Dunn!

                    JD
          Nice!

A beat.

                    JD
          Don't change the subject. Nice try.

                    BERNADETTE
          You want I should go rescue your
          cat?

                    JD
          Please.

Bernadette runs upstairs.

                    BERNADETTE (O.S.)
          Hey! Bad dog! No! Ow!

JD LAUGHS and calls upstairs.

                    JD
          Good dog! I think I'll name him
          Bitey!

                    BERNADETTE (O.S.)
          I'm doing this for you, ya know!

JD sits down and watches Dragonball GT on TV.

Bill walks in, covered in mud.

                    EDNA
          I'll get you a towel.

                    BILL
          Make it a Screwdriver.

                    BERNADETTE (O.S.)
          Ow!

Everybody stops and looks at the staircase.

                    BERNADETTE (O.S.)
          Everything's okay!

JD goes back to the TV, while his parents continue their
conversation.

                    BILL
          Everything all right in here?

Spiffy runs down the stairs and across the living room.
Scooby Dunn follows close behind.

                    SCOOBY
          WOOF! WOOF! WOOF! WOOF! WOOF!

                    EDNA
          Does that answer your question?

                    BILL
          I think I'll have a double.

INT. HARTFORD HIGH SCHOOL - MUSIC CLASS - AFTERNOON

JD and Nick talk while composing a song. Mr. Speigel stands
over other groups' shoulders, monitoring their progress.

                    JD
          He finally stopped barking at two
          in the morning.

                    NICK
          Damn. It sounds like she's at least
          trying to make amends.

                    JD
          We'll see how long that lasts.

                    NICK
          Ready for the show tomorrow night?

                    JD
          You know it!

                    NICK
          There's no second chance at this.
          Are you okay with that?

                    JD
          We'll be fine.

                                        CUT TO:

INT. BROCK TRENT'S OFFICE - EVENING

Brock sits on the phone with his feet on his desk.

                    BROCK
          Yes, and I want the same conditions
          as we have for his father... Good.
          I'll have him look over the
          contract after tomorrow night's
          performance... All he has to do is
          show up and perform. You won't be
          disappointed... Okay, I'll talk to
          you tomorrow night at the show.

Brock puts his phone down, and writes himself a memo.

ANGLE: THE MEMO: JUDE DUNN CONTRACT DEAL.

Brock slides the memo in a file folder marked NITRO PUMPKINS
and takes the folder with him out of the office.

He turns out the lights and closes the door behind him.

INT. HARTFORD HIGH SCHOOL - HALLWAY - AFTERNOON

The bell RINGS, and students crowd the hallway on their way
home for the day.

JD walks up to his locker, looking around. Brendan walks up.

                    JD
          Hey, have you seen Amy?

                    BRENDAN
          I've been looking for Nick.

                    JD
          That's odd.

JD and Brendan walk around the corner to Nick's locker.

ANGLE: RICKY KISSES AMY AT NICK'S LOCKER.

JD turns around and storms off in a huff. Brendan stays
behind a moment, looking back and forth at JD and Ricky.

                    BRENDAN
          Oh, jeez.

INT. HARTFORD HIGH SCHOOL - AUDITORIUM - MOMENTS LATER

JD passes by the auditorium, angry as can be. Asher runs out
of the auditorium and grabs JD.

                    ASHER
          Dude! There you are! Have you seen
          Nick? Ricky's supposed to be here,
          too.

                    JD
          I haven't seen Nick, but tell Ricky
          he can suck off when he's done
          sucking Amy's face.

Asher's face crinkles.

                    ASHER
          What?

                    JD
          Forget it. I'm done.

                    ASHER
          What's wrong?

Ricky and Amy walk up to the auditorium. They instantly
notice JD's mood.

                    RICKY
          What happened? JD, why are you so
          upset?

                    JD
          You know why.

                    AMY
          No. We don't. Jude, tell us.

Amy reaches out to put her hand on JD's shoulder, but he
swats it away.

                    AMY
          Jude!

                    JD
          I saw you two kissing earlier.

                    AMY
          I don't understand.

                    RICKY
          What are you talking about?

                    JD
          I'm talking about when you were at
          Nick's locker after school.

                    RICKY
          Oh, that? It was just a joke.

                    JD
          Don't lie to me!

                    AMY
          We really should tell him, Ricky.

                    JD
          Tell me what?

                    AMY
          Ricky is my boyfriend now.

Nick walks up to the auditorium.

                    NICK
          Hey, what's going on?

                    JD
          Bite me! I'm out!

                    NICK
          What? Hakuna matata, remember?

                    JD
          Fuck you all! How many of you knew
          about this?

                    AMY
          Nobody. We kinda kept it a
          secret... from... well, everybody,
          really.

                    JD
          Get bent! I'm done!

                    NICK
          JD, don't do this. If we don't go
          on, we forfeit the show. You were
          so excited.

                    ASHER
          If you leave now, John will...

                    NICK
          Stay out of this, Asher!

A beat.

                    JD
          No, hold on! John Hammel will what?

                    NICK
          Don't answer that.

                    ASHER
          If you leave, John will lord it
          over our heads that we kicked him
          out of the band.

Nick cringes.

                    JD
          You lied to me? You told me that he
          quit the band!

                    NICK
          No, I... I kicked him out and he
          bet me our spot in the show that
          we'd come begging for him back.
          Please, JD. Don't let him win.

                    JD
          You bet what?

                    NICK
          I thought you'd want to stick him
          on this. I'm... I'm sorry.

                    JD
          Stick this!

JD flicks off Nick and storms out the side door to the
school.

                    NICK
          JD! Shit!

                    AMY
          Want me to go talk to him?

                    NICK
          No, he's mad at all of us.

                    ASHER
          What do we do? Show's gotta go on.

                    NICK
          Keep going as if nothing happened
          and hope he calms down in time.

                    ASHER
          We have three hours before the
          show; that's not enough time.

INT. THE DUNNS' LIVING ROOM - EVENING

JD sulks on the living room couch. Tears roll down his face,
but he's dead silent. Bernadette walks into the room.

                    BERNADETTE
          Hey, it's almost time for your
          show. Aren't you going to get
          ready.

JD sulks.

                    BERNADETTE
          I don't know what happened, but is
          this how you want to be remembered?
          As a temperamental Aspie whose
          emotions control him?

JD sulks.

                    BERNADETTE
          Can you look at me?

JD sulks and looks Bernadette in the eye.

                    BERNADETTE
          This is your big chance to show
          everyone what an Aspie can do. This
          is your Cell.

                    JD
          What?

                    BERNADETTE
          I know I'm gonna regret this, but
          do you remember Gohan from
          Dragonball Z.

                    JD
          Yeah, but...

                    BERNADETTE
          The greatest thing he ever did was
          beat Cell, right?

                    JD
          Yeah...

                    BERNADETTE
          Don't you see? You're Gohan, and
          the show is your Cell. You have to
          win the talent show.

A beat.

                    JD
          I didn't think you watched DBZ.

                    BERNADETTE
          Are you kidding? You made me watch
          it with you all throughout your
          childhood.

Somebody KNOCKS on the front door.

                    BERNADETTE
          Care to answer it?

JD opens the front door. Ricky stands outside before him.

                    RICKY
          JD, you're coming with me, and I
          don't want any trouble.

Ricky puts his fists up, ready to block a punch.

                    JD
          Let me get my guitar.

Ricky drops his hands in confusion.

                    RICKY
          Wait, what? It worked that easily?

                    JD
          Gotta beat Cell.

                    RICKY
          God, I don't understand you.

                    JD
          Good. Neither do I.

INT. HARTFORD HIGH SCHOOL - AUDITORIUM - LATER

The Nitro Pumpkins stand backstage, waiting. Nick walks up to
his bandmates.

                    NICK
          Still no sign of Ricky and JD.

                    ASHER
          But we go on in less than three
          minutes!

                    BRENDAN
          We're out of time.

                    NICK
          We'll just have to go on without a
          guitarist.

                    ASHER
          That's suicide!

                    NICK
          It's the only thing we can do.

EXT. HARTFORD HIGH SCHOOL - PARKING LOT - MOMENTS LATER

A blue Honda Accord pulls into a spot. Ricky and JD jump out
of the car and run toward the school, guitar in hand.

                    RICKY
          Hurry up!

INT. HARTFORD HIGH SCHOOL - AUDITORIUM - MOMENTS LATER

Mr. Speigel walks up to the Nitro Pumpkins.

                    MR. SPEIGEL
          You guys are on. You ready? Where's
          JD?

                    NICK
          We're going on without him.

                    MR. SPEIGEL
          Okay, just do your best.

                    NICK
          We will.

INT. HARTFORD HIGH SCHOOL - HALLWAY - MOMENTS LATER

JD and Ricky run toward the auditorium.

                    JD
          I'm telling you, it's this way! I
          would know!

                    RICKY
          Fine. Just don't stop running.

INT. HARTFORD HIGH SCHOOL - AUDITORIUM - MOMENTS LATER

The Nitro Pumpkins minus JD cross the stage. The crowd
CHEERS.

Someone in the crowd shouts at the stage.

                    STUDENT #1
          Hey! Where's JD?

                    STUDENT #2
          Yeah! We want JD!

The crowd starts chanting.

                    CROWD
          JD! JD! JD! JD!

Asher pulls Nick aside.

                    ASHER
          This is bad. They want JD. We're
          gonna lose them.

                    NICK
          I'm aware of that. Just act
          natural.

ANGLE: SOMEBODY PLUGS IN AN AMP BACKSTAGE.

Nick closes his eyes, and braces himself to start to play.

                    NICK
          Here goes...

Before the band can play, the guitar riff from Dire Straits'
"Money for Nothing" ECHOES across the auditorium. The crowd
stops chanting and CHEERS again.

Nick looks up to see JD playing the riff.

                    NICK
          JD.

                    JD
          That's your cue, Pumbaa. Hakuna
          matata.

Nick smiles and motions for the band to start over.

                    JD
          What's my name?

                    CROWD
          JD!

                    JD
          I can't hear you!

                    CROWD
               (louder)
          JD!

                    JD
          Louder!

                    CROWD
               (still louder)
          JD!

                    JD
          Say it loud! Say it proud!

JD starts the riff over, and the band picks up on cue this
time.

MONTAGE:

The Nitro Pumpkins play their best set they've ever played.

The crowd lights up and screams at the Nitro Pumpkins.

JD jumps into the audience and rocks out, encouraging the
crowd to rock out with him.

John Hammel stands, sulking. Another student in the audience
nudges him. John turns around and walks out.

JD steps back up on stage for the big finish.

                    JD
          I know we said our platform was
          Autism Awareness, but we just
          wanted to dedicate that song we
          just played to a very special
          friend of ours. She lost her mother
          to cancer this past year, and we
          wanted her to know that we care.
          Thank you!

Amy holds back tears in the audience.

The crowd CHEERS and starts a new chant.

                    CROWD
          ENCORE! ENCORE! ENCORE! ENCORE!

JD turns to Nick.

                    JD
          Sorry about earlier.

                    NICK
          Not a problem. Just don't do that
          again. We need you; you're a vital
          part of this band.

ANGLE: THE JUDGES SCRIBBLE ON A PAPER AND PASS IT OVER TO
BROCK.

Brock takes the stage, waving the paper in his hand.

                    BROCK
          You guys want an encore?

                    CROWD
          YEAH!

                    BROCK
          Well, how about this for an encore?
          I'm holding in my hand a contract
          with FME Records signed by my
          colleagues and myself. How many of
          you guys think the Nitro Pumpkins
          deserve this contract.

The crowd SCREAMS louder than before.

                    BROCK
          How about it guys? The crowd seems
          to think you deserve it. What do
          you think?

The band huddles a moment then breaks.

                    JD
          How do we know we're not getting
          screwed?

                    BROCK
          JD, my boy, we're prepared to give
          you the exact same deal your father
          has. He's already given us the
          okay. If you want, you can talk to
          him after the show.

                    JD
          I think we'll do that.

                    BROCK
          Let the negotiations begin!

The crowd SCREAMS again.

                    BROCK
          Settle down, people! We need a few
          minutes to score the bands. We'll
          be right back after a ten minute
          intermission to reveal the winners.

The audience migrates to...

THE HALLWAY

Bernadette, Bill, and Edna stand outside the auditorium. Mr.
D. walks up.

                    MR. D.
          I'm proud of JD. You all should be,
          too.

                    BILL
          Brock contacted me about giving
          Jude a contract. Who's idea was it?

                    MR. D.
          It wasn't me. That much, I can tell
          you.

                    BERNADETTE
          If it wasn't you, and it wasn't my
          dad, then who was it?

                    MR. D.
          I can't tell you that.

Behind them, Jack Gladwynne talks with Brock.

                    BROCK
          They loved him out there! The
          contract was a great idea.

                    JACK GLADWYNNE
          Yeah, well. I think this works out
          better, no matter how it ends.

Mr. D. walks past Brock and Jack Gladwynne.

                    MR. D.
          They're onto us.

Mr. D. smiles.

                    JACK GLADWYNNE
          I'll handle that.

Bill greets Brock.

                    BILL
          Hey, Brock. I see you met my
          neighbor, Jack.

                    JACK GLADWYNNE
          We were just talking about how
          great Jude did out there.

                    BILL
          I suppose I owe you a giant thank
          you.

                    JACK GLADWYNNE
          You don't need to thank me for
          anything. He earned it out there.

                    BILL
          He sure did!

                    BROCK
          I'm telling you, Billy, your son is
          going to go far. You've raised a
          modern day Mozart.

Bill laughs.

                    BILL
          I'll tell him you said that.

Bill starts to walk away.

                    BILL
          Oh, and your secret's safe with me,
          guys.

Jack Gladwynne chuckles.

                    JACK GLADWYNNE
          All right, then. Hey, isn't it
          about time to announce the winners?

                    BILL
          Eh, I'll go back in a few minutes.

INT. HARTFORD HIGH SCHOOL - AUDITORIUM - LATER

Bill sits down with his family, chuckling.

                    EDNA
          Well?

                    BILL
          Well, what?

                    BERNADETTE
          Who was it? You know something
          don't you?

Amy returns just in time for the conversation.

                    BILL
          I don't know anything.

Bill winks at Amy. Amy smiles.

                    EDNA
          That's for sure. Give your uncle my
          thanks, Amy.

Bill and Amy startle.

                    BILL
          You knew?

                    EDNA
          You didn't think he had the idea on
          his own, did you?

Edna winks back at Bill.

                    BILL
          You're just evil, aren't you?

                    EDNA
          I was going to tell you when we got
          home.

                    BILL
          Definitely evil.

                    BERNADETTE
          You raised a son whose dream when
          he was six was to build a death ray
          and destroy the sun. I think you
          both qualify as "evil."

                    BILL
          Watch your mouth. We prefer the
          term "heroically impaired" in this
          house, young lady.

                    BERNADETTE
          No wonder Jude's a dork.

                    EDNA
          Bernie!

                    BERNADETTE
          What? He's our dork.

                    EDNA
          And we wouldn't want him any other
          way.

Bill and Amy look at...

THE STAGE

Brock returns with the microphone.

                    BROCK
          Okay, ladies and gentlemen! It's
          the moment we're all here for! The
          three bands moving on to VH1's "New
          Classics" reality show are...

ANGLE: THE NITRO PUMPKINS LOOK ON AT THE EDGE OF THEIR SEATS.

ANGLE: JOHN HAMMEL ROLLS HIS EYES.

ANGLE: RICKY AND AMY LOOK AT EACH OTHER, THEN AT BROCK.

                    BROCK
          Climbing Disasters!

The crowd CHEERS.

ANGLE: BILL WINCES.

                    BROCK
          The Buzz Fuzz!

ANGLE: JOHN HAMMEL SMIRKS.

ANGLE: JD WETS HIS LIPS.

                    BROCK
          And... the biggest winner of all...

ANGLE: JD LEANS FORWARD.

                    BROCK
          The Nitro Pumpkins!

The crowd SCREAMS louder than any previous screaming
combined.

ANGLE: JD FALLS OUT OF HIS SEAT.

                    BROCK
          Congratulations, New Classics! Stay
          tuned to VH1 this fall for the two
          hour premiere!

The rest of Brock's speech is overpowered by the SOUNDS OF
APPLAUSE, CHEERING, AND THUNDER.

EXT. HARTFORD HIGH SCHOOL - PARKING LOT - NIGHT

People migrate back to their cars, as John Hammel makes a
scene.

Security personnel escort John Hammel out of the building.

                    JOHN
          You can't do this! This isn't
          right! He's an Aspie! Why are you
          all enabling him!

Brock pokes his head out the door.

                    BROCK
          Just get that brat out of here!

                    JOHN
          Who are you calling a brat, old
          man?

The Dunns approach their car. The Nitro Pumpkins sign their
contract behind them.

                    BILL
          It turned out even better than we
          could have hoped.

                    BERNADETTE
          Do you have any idea what this is
          going to do to his ego?

JD comes running up to the car.

                    JD
          Stuff it, Bern! I'm a rock star,
          now! Bow to the Prince of All Rock
          Stars!

                    BERNADETTE
          You can stop with the DBZ metaphors
          now. It only worked the first time.

                    JD
          You missed out on four years of
          this stuff. Just trying to catch
          you up.

                    BERNADETTE
          Dear lord!

Bernadette slams her door shut.

Amy walks by.

                    JD
          Hey, mind if I walk home, tonight?

                    EDNA
          I don't know...

                    BILL
          Ah, let him go, Edna. He's earned
          it, and it's not that far.

                    EDNA
          Oh, okay. We'll leave the door
          unlocked for you.

                    JD
          Thanks.

EXT. SENTRY RD. - MOMENTS LATER

JD runs up behind Amy.

                    JD
          Hey, got a minute?

                    AMY
          You're not still mad, are you?

                    JD
          About that... I guess I
          overreacted. The truth is...

A beat.

                    JD
          The truth is I love you.

Amy stops walking.

                    AMY
          Jude.

                    JD
          The fact of the matter is you
          deserve someone who can make you
          happy, and I'm not going to be
          around to be able to do that.

                    AMY
          So, what are you saying?

                    JD
          I love you, Amy, but I have to let
          go. I just wanted you to know how I
          feel. You have a whole year left to
          figure yourself out. I'm going to
          UCLA in the fall. FME's paying for
          it. Point is...

A beat.

                    JD
          Point is I want you to be happy. If
          that means dating Ricky, then...
          Then so be it.

                    AMY
          Jude. I don't know what to say.

                    JD
          You don't have to say anything.

                    AMY
          Thank you. You'll find somebody,
          I'm sure.

                    JD
          Thank you.

The two share a hug and continue walking home.

                    JD
          So, did you see John get kicked out
          by Brock at the end?

                    AMY
          No way! You're so making that up.

                    JD
          I'm so not making it up. He took a
          swing at Brock backstage.

JD and Amy trail off along with the sound of their voices.

                                        DISSOLVE TO:

INT. HARTFORD HIGH SCHOOL - MR. D.'S CLASS - AFTERNOON

Mr. D. picks up his briefcase, as students leave the room.

JD and Ricky walk in. Mr. D. doesn't even pick his head up.

                    MR. D.
          You graduated two days ago, boys.
          There's nothing left for me to
          teach you.

                    JD
          Don't you have any last words for
          us?

                    RICKY
          Yeah, like a final word of wisdom
          from our favorite teacher?

Mr. D. puts down his briefcase and sits down at his desk.

JD and Ricky sit down before him.

                    MR. D.
          You have come farther than either
          of you will ever comprehend.

                    JD
          Can we skip past this part. I've
          been hearing it all month.

                    MR. D.
          Very well. I'll give you guys
          something more tangible to ponder.

                    JD
          World's a scary place. Tangible
          would help.

                    MR. D.
          And men like you will surely make
          it a less scary place to be.

                    RICKY
          Even me?

                    MR. D.
          Yes, Mr. Mallo. There's even hope
          for you. My advice to you is
          simple. Love much. Try hard. Dream
          big. Never give in to the side of
          you that tells you otherwise. Say
          to yourselves, if you have to: I am
          me. I am the only me there will
          ever be. I am the best me I can be.
          Things may not always go my way,
          and I am okay with that. I'm doing
          my best, and that's what really
          matters.

                    JD
          What if our best isn't enough?

                    MR. D.
          If it's truly your best, it will be
          enough, Mr. Dunn. Be the change you
          want to see in the world. Do that
          much, and you won't have any
          regrets.

JD and Ricky turn around to leave. JD stops at the door.

                    JD
          Thank you.

Mr. D. waves, and JD exits the classroom.

                    MR. D.
          You're welcome.

                                        DISSOLVE TO:

INT. THE DUNNS' LIVING ROOM - NIGHT

Edna, Bernadette, Ricky, and the Gladwynnes sit on the couch
watching the TV.

Amy sits next to Ricky, his arm around her on the couch.

Edna picks up the remote.

                    EDNA
          Ooh! Everyone be quiet; the show's
          back on.

ANGLE: THE TV SCREEN.

INSERT: VH1 PRESENTS: NEW CLASSICS

JD sits in a chair, talking into the camera during an
interview.

                    INTERVIEWER (O.S.)
          Some people look at you and how far
          you've come with a guitar in just
          one year, and they say, "I want to
          be like him." What advice do you
          have for them?

                    JD
          Try your damnedest. If you don't
          ever try, you're never going to
          succeed.

                    INTERVIEWER (O.S.)
          Has this newfound fame spoiled you
          in any way? Sex, drugs, rock and
          roll?

                    JD
          Just the rock and roll. Which I
          love more than sex and consume like
          a drug, so I guess that's three for
          three.

The group watching on the couch LAUGH.

                    EDNA
          I can't believe he said that on
          national TV.

                    BERNADETTE
          Shush!

ANGLE: TV SCREEN.

                    JD
          Seriously, though, I'm trying to
          limit that kind of junk. I'm trying
          to set a positive example for other
          Aspies out there.

                    INTERVIEWER (O.S.)
          Yes, you're doing a very good job!
          Tell me, is there anything in
          particular you'd like to say to
          anyone?

                    JD
          Just that...

JD pauses.

                    JD
          Just that no matter how much life
          knocks you down, you have to keep
          getting back up. You can meet 99
          people in your life who will knock
          you down, but it's the hope that
          number 100 will help you up that
          has to keep motivating you. If you
          don't take any chances, you'll
          never know what could have been.
          And if 100 does help you, it makes
          everything worthwhile. You'll never
          know if you don't try.

                    INTERVIEWER (O.S.)
          That's very sage of you.

                    JD
          Someone, somewhere once said that
          you have to earn your soul. I feel
          that's true in every possible way.

                    INTERVIEWER (O.S.)
          You've definitely earned yours.
          This has been Jude Dunn from the
          Nitro Pumpkins, and you're watching
          New Classics on VH1. We'll be right
          back with some live concert footage
          of Wild Billy and the Maniacs in
          Atlanta after this.

Back to the couch.

                    AMY
          You know, he's very wise for
          someone his age.

                    JACK GLADWYNNE
          I think you helped him become that
          wise.

                    AMY
          No.

                    EDNA
          No, really. You did wonders for
          him.

                    AMY
          You think?

                    RICKY
          We know so.

Ricky holds Amy's hand. Amy responds with a peck on the
cheek.

                    BERNADETTE
          I wonder what he's doing now?

EXT. UCLA - GRASSY HILL - EVENING

JD sits under a tree, strumming on an electric-acoustic
guitar.

The sunset blankets him in a warm glow.

ANOTHER STUDENT, 18, walks up with a set of bongos. JD stops
playing.

                    JD
I'm sorry, did I disturb you?

                  ASHLEY
No, not at all! My name's Ashley.

                    JD
Jude, but you can call me JD if you
want.

                  ASHLEY
Mind if I jam with you, JD?

                    JD
I'd be insulted if you didn't!

                  ASHLEY
That's a nice sunset.

                    JD
It's beautiful.

                  ASHLEY
So, where are you from? I'm from
Arizona.

                    JD
I'm from Pennsylvania.

                  ASHLEY
Wait! Are you the guy from the
Nitro Pumpkins?

                    JD
Yeah! That's my band. We're all
here on campus. FME pays for our
education.

                  ASHLEY
I'm so jealous! My bandmates
ditched me for community college.
Even my boyfriend ditched me.

                    JD
So sorry to hear that.

                  ASHLEY
Yeah, well, I just broke up with
him, anyway.

                    JD
That's too sad.

                    ASHLEY
          Nah, he cheated on me. He tried to
          hide it at first, but I caught him.
          I'm not upset at all. I'm actually
          feeling kinda... liberated.

JD starts strumming his guitar again. Ashley plays her
bongos.

                    JD
          That's good. I bet that feels so
          much better.

                    ASHLEY
          Oh, it does.

                    JD
          Wanna hit up the Welcome Week
          concert tomorrow night?

                    ASHLEY
          I'd love to.

The two jam out as the sun sinks lower in the Western sky.

INT. THE DUNNS' LIVING ROOM - NIGHT

The group still watches the TV, their heads all tilted to the
side as if in a daydream.

                    BERNADETTE
          I'm sure he'll be fine. How much
          trouble can he get into in
          California? Right?

The rest of the group look at her like they've seen a ghost.

                    BERNADETTE
          Right... I'll get the phone.

                    EDNA
          Thank you, Sweetie.

                                        FADE TO:

EXT. UCLA - GRASSY HILL - NIGHT

The sun has long set, and a gibbous moon is bright in the
night sky.

JD and Ashley still jam out under the tree.

                    ASHLEY
          I'm hungry. Is the song over yet?

                    JD
          It's not over until one of us
          stops.

Ashley stops playing her bongos and stands up.

                    ASHLEY
          It's over.

                              FADE TO BLACK.